BEST
FRENEMIES
FOREVER

BEST FRENEMIES FOREVER

MEGAN McCAFFERTY

Scholastic Press • New York

All rights reserved. Published by Scholastic Press, an imprint of Scholastic Inc., *Publishers since 1920*. SCHOLASTIC, SCHOLASTIC PRESS, and associated logos are trademarks and/or registered trademarks of Scholastic Inc.

The publisher does not have any control over and does not assume any responsibility for author or third-party websites or their content.

This book is a work of fiction. Names, characters, places, and incidents are either the product of the author's imagination or are used fictitiously, and any resemblance to actual persons, living or dead, business establishments, events, or locales is entirely coincidental.

Library of Congress Cataloging-in-Publication Data available

ISBN 978-1-338-72249-9

1 2021

Printed in the U.S.A.   23

First edition, March 2022

Book design by Yaffa Jaskoll

To Caitlyn, Collin, Carly, Zoë, Cailey, and Max,
for keeping me young(ish)

PART ONE

THE NEW GIRL

THE NEW GIRL MOVED IN NEXT DOOR WHILE WE WERE ON VACATION.
Mom is making me introduce myself.

"She's from Virginia and doesn't know anyone," Mom says. "I bet she's bored and lonely."

I've lived in New Jersey my whole life. I know everyone. It's the last week of summer vacation and I'm as bored and lonely as anyone could be.

Mom's family visited the same beach house when she was my age. We inherited it after my grandparents retired to Florida three years ago. Dad says we should get as much use out of it now as we possibly can before it's totally underwater with the rest of the Jersey Shore. It's not big or fancy, but it's right across the street from a bird sanctuary, one block from the ocean, and three doors down from the summer home of international pop star Riley Quick.

I'm not making this up.

When I made the mistake of sharing this information with Morgan Middleton last year, she snorted and rolled her eyes and told everyone I was a liar. Even my former best friend, Ella—who just a few months earlier had happily posed for photos in front of Riley Quick's house—agreed that I'd made it all up just to get attention.

But it's true. Mostly true. Riley Quick *did* spend her summers at a beach house three doors down from mine. And everyone in Pebble Harbor still calls it Riley Quick's House. Unfortunately I was never in town at the same time as Riley Quick. She stopped vacationing there the year I was born because she got too rich and famous for the Jersey Shore. This is just my kind of bad luck.

I think it might be worth mentioning it to the New Girl, though.

The New Girl looks like the beachy, ponytailed type interested in Riley Quick, summers at the shore, or both. She's dressed in denim shorts and layered tank tops like all the other girls do between June and August. The New Girl has knotted her pink and purple tanks at the hip. This isn't how girls around here wear them. Maybe that's the style in Virginia? I don't wear tank tops because I'm pale skinned like my Celtic, foggy bog–dwelling ancestors. My parents won't let me leave the house until I put on a long-sleeved, UVA- and UVB-blocking button-down that is more high-tech than trendy.

I can't see the New Girl's face. She's walking on her hands across the grass, just casually making her way from one side of the lawn to the other, as if using her arms as legs is the easiest way to get around. I wait to say "hey" because I don't want to startle her and take the blame for making her crash. I silently watch her for a few more seconds before she flips forward and lands on her feet.

"Hey!" she says, beating me to it.

Her face is red. All the blood must have rushed to her head when she was upside down. This can put a dangerous strain on the heart. The New Girl doesn't seem at all concerned about this and I remind myself it's not my job to get worried for her. The New Girl's face is swiftly changing back to the same sun-kissed color as the rest of her body. Her arms and legs are tanned, her honey-brown hair is scattered with golden highlights. Her parents must not encourage her to apply and reapply sunscreen, the safest kind that's made with titanium dioxide and thicker than paste. If she does wear sunscreen, it probably contains dangerous chemicals covered up with a coconut scent. This carefree attitude about safe sun protection will give Dad another reason to disapprove of the New Girl's family.

The New Girl is studying me with a familiar curious look. As usual, my mind is working faster than my mouth and she's waiting for me to speak up.

"Hey!"

It seems like the safest thing to say.

APPROACHABLE PRETTY

BECAUSE SHE'S A GIRL AND I'M A GIRL AND MORGANELLA HAS SORT of brainwashed me to think such things important even though Mom has raised me to think they are not, let's get this out of the way: The New Girl is pretty. Obviously prettier than me. When I look at myself, I see a cut-and-paste collage of inherited traits. I get fair skin, black hair, and wide-set gray eyes from Mom. Thin-lipped mouth, skinny legs, and narrow build from Dad. Pointy arrow nose from mystery relatives I've never met.

I don't mind that the New Girl is prettier than I am because I don't try very hard to be pretty. MorganElla says any girl who gets her hair cut to her earlobes isn't trying *at all*. The New Girl is also prettier than Morgan, who tries very hard to turn her pinched face into prettiness. She's maybe even prettier than Ella, who was the prettiest girl at Shadybrook Elementary School and might still be the prettiest girl when we get to Mercer Middle School. Ella has turned into a snotty, toss-her-shiny-hair-turn-up-her-button-nose-roll-her-hazel-eyes kind of pretty though. The kind of pretty that can ruin your whole day.

I don't like saying this about my ex–best friend but it's true.

The New Girl is a more approachable kind of pretty. Her large brown eyes are warm and welcoming. Dimples hug her bright smile. Her nose doesn't make me nervous. I mean, not any more nervous than I already am on any other ordinary day.

My parents think I'm stressed out because I'm super-overscheduled during the school year with too much homework and FUNdamentals of Science Club and Girl Scouts and what used to be called playdates but is now just called "hanging out." They solved that problem by not signing me up for any summer camps but didn't seem to realize that boredom had its own challenges. This is why I took matters into my own hands and gave myself 100 Things To Do.

THE BOOK OF AWESOME FOR AWESOME GIRLS

Hey, Girls!

Are you ready to be your best self? We crossed continents, scoured history books, and asked top experts to put together this ultimate girl's guide to gutsiness and getting things done. Can you build a life raft? Make a clock that runs on lemons? Design a totally cute T-shirt? Our answer: YES YOU CAN. This carefully cultivated To Do List of projects, crafts, and challenges is designed to get you out of your comfort zone and into the awesome zone!

So unplug from technology and unglue your eyes from the screen. Discover skills you never knew you had! Tap into hidden talents and dazzle the world! Whether you tackle them in order or jump around, crossing off these To Dos is guaranteed to give you a Can-Do Attitude that will last long after you've finished number 100. And with the confidence to say yes to new experiences, you'll never be bored again.

Remember: Awesome girls aren't born that way, they're made! You are the next generation of creatives, fixers, and leaders. Start your journey toward awesomeness today!

The Awesome Girls Team

K–A–Y–T–E–E

MOM SAYS I SHOULD TALK ABOUT MY FEELINGS WHEN I'M anxious. But it's not like I can come right out and tell the New Girl about my To Do List because that would be too weird too soon. That's why most of my best conversations happen inside my own head. And most of the worst ones too.

The New Girl squints to get a better look at me.

"You're the girl my age who lives next door."

I nod.

"I heard about you."

Five seconds into my first conversation with the New Girl and I'm already failing at being normal. I try the breathing technique Mom taught me to calm nervous heartpang when it hits:

Inhale.

Expand the belly.

Count to three.

Exhale.

Squeeze the belly.

Count to three.

I do the breathing technique, but my words still come out all short, staccato, stuttered. That never happens inside my head.

"What did you hear?"

"I heard." The New Girl motions for me to come closer. "That you're *a girl my age who lives next door!*"

She slaps her cheeks dramatically.

"Scandal!"

It takes me a moment or two to get that she's making a joke. She hasn't heard anything about me. Yet.

"So," she says. "What did *you* hear about *me?*"

She curls her hands under her chin and looks up at me with a similar kind of exaggerated cutie-pie pouty face as Ella makes in all her selfies.

"I heard." I motion for the New Girl to come closer. "That you're a girl my age who lives next door."

Then *I* slap *my* cheeks dramatically.

"Scandal!"

The joke isn't as funny when I do it because we've both heard it already. Also, I don't have the New Girl's comic flair. The punch line comes out flat and I slap my cheeks a little too hard. Despite the flaws in my delivery, the New Girl still smiles at me in a satisfied way.

"My name's Kaytee Ray, just like Kaytee K.," she says. "I spell it the same way too. K-A-Y-T-E-E."

Oh well. So much for impressing the New Girl with the beach house. As everyone knows, Kaytee K. and Riley Quick are total frenemies. Fans pick one pop princess or the other and there's no going back. Kayters versus Ribots. It's good to know early on where the New Girl stands.

"Something wrong?" Kaytee asks.

"No, I'm Sophie, just like . . ."

Sophie Germain is the first famous Sophie who comes to mind. "Research Another Awesome Girl with Your Same Name" was number 21 on my To Do List. I was pretty proud of how I handled that To Do. It could've been completed in just a few quick clicks on the laptop, over and done in seconds. But my initial Google search led me to the second floor of the public library, where I spent almost four hours with a stack of biographies and nonfiction to find out more about her. I could tell Kaytee that Sophie Germain was a French mathematician, physicist, and philosopher who died over 150 years ago, but I won't. Talking about dead trailblazing feminists definitely falls under the category of "weird things to say."

There were three Sophies in my grade at Shadybrook Elementary—two with *ph*'s and one with an *f*—and who knows how many more there will be when I start Mercer Middle School? Kaytee doesn't know any of those girls so it makes no sense for me to share that information either, though I come very close to sharing it anyway because it's awkward just standing there. Fortunately Kaytee has enough to say for the two of us.

"How old are you?" she asks.

"Twelve."

Kaytee eyes me doubtfully. I make a quick correction.

"Well, almost."

"Hooooow almost twelve are you?" Kaytee teases.

"My birthday is next month . . ."

She claps energetically.

"Mine too! When's yours?"

"September twenty-second."

"Stop it." She pushes me in a playful way that is surprisingly powerful considering she's two or three inches shorter than I am. "My birthday is September twenty-third! Are you going into sixth or seventh grade?"

"Seventh," I say.

"Me too!" She hops around in a little circle. "We're both the babies of our grade!"

It takes a moment to realize she's not making fun of me. She's just pointing out the truth: We were both born just before the October first deadline, making us the last to turn twelve before everyone else starts turning thirteen. Until recently I would've said we're built similarly: straight lined and flat chested. In the past few months I guess I filled out a little bit. Enough for Mom to sit me down for awkward talks about "breast tenderness" I didn't want to listen to. Enough for her to buy a bra I didn't want to try on.

* * *

I'd still be wearing a cami under my shirts if I hadn't overheard Morgan talking about me in the girls' room. It was one of the last days of sixth grade and I had just presented my end-of-the-year science report on climate change, rising sea levels, and beach erosion.

"She's always going on about the end of the planet in her know-it-all voice." I watched Morgan fluff her attention-getting red hair through the crack in the bathroom door. "She thinks she's so much more mature than we are! But *she's* the one wearing a toddler undershirt!"

Morgan didn't know I was in the stall. She didn't say it to hurt my feelings. She said it to make Ella—who I couldn't see but was, as always, standing right next to her—laugh. She succeeded at both. After ten months of practice, Morgan knew the easiest way to make Ella laugh was for the joke to be on me.

There were only two days left in sixth grade and I put on my new bra for both of them. It was scratchy and uncomfortable, but I'd never be caught wearing a toddler undershirt again. I knew I'd never get approval from Morgan. But even after all the rejection I'd endured all year, I still pathetically held out for some sort of acknowledgment from Ella.

It didn't come.

Kaytee's wearing a bra underneath her tank tops, even though she doesn't have much to support. I wonder if she was mocked back in Virginia for wearing toddler undershirts.

I wonder if she's still waiting to get her first period.

I wonder if she's afraid everyone is growing up and leaving her behind.

I wonder if she's convinced everything she thinks and does and says is all wrong—which is ironic when you're mocked as a know-it-all.

I doubt it.

The New Girl is still beaming over this news, this unexpected something we have in common.

"September birthdays! Holla!"

Kaytee Ray definitely lives up to her radiant last name.

She removes a tube of lip gloss from her front pocket and makes an O with her mouth to apply it. Then she does something surprising: She offers the wand to me! We just met! For all she knows, I could have a weird mouth fungus undetectable by the naked eye.

For all I know, so could she.

Again, I doubt it.

"Want some?" she asks. "This color would look awesome on you."

The gloss is a vivid raspberry Mom would say is too bold for a girl with my complexion. Not that it matters anyway because she doesn't believe in makeup before the age of thirteen. She's a social worker and says too many clients end up in her office because they're in a rush to grow up too soon.

"No thanks," I say. "I'm just getting over a cold. I don't want you to get it."

"Ick! Ack! Ick!" Kaytee cries out.

The grin on her face says she's kidding. But too often it's too hard for me to tell.

ICKFACE

SIXTH GRADE ENDED IN THE TOILET. BUT IT BEGAN IN THE CHOIR room.

"Umm. Is it, like, even possible for her to sing without making ickface?"

Morgan wasn't subtle. She leaned right in front of me to steal my best friend.

"Nope," Ella replied with a wicked giggle. "Ickface *is* her face."

I was standing right next to her on the border between the altos and the sopranos when she, Ella, my best friend since kindergarten, said it. I didn't realize it then, but that's the moment the two girls formerly known as Morgan and Ella became the two-faced, single-brained girlbeast known as MorganElla. The transformation was instantaneous. I never saw it coming. That's why I stupidly assumed Ella was still joking *with* me and not *at* me. I laughed right along with them.

Just to be sure, I tried to catch myself making ickface as I practiced harmonies in the bathroom mirror at home. I didn't see anything icky about it. When I reported the absence of ickface at the next music class, the Morgan-headed half of the monster MorganElla rolled her eyes and ummmed at me.

"Ummm. That's because you're tragically blind to your own flaws!"

That time when Ella laughed, there was a harshness, a *mean-ness* I'd never heard before. Who was this person? Where was the girl who had slept over at my house hundreds of times between kindergarten and the summer before sixth grade? Why was my best friend suddenly a bigger danger than any stranger? Months later, when Ella's harsher, meaner laughter echoed in the girls' bathroom, it was more familiar to me than any memory of the friendship we'd once had.

I hear Morgan's ummms in my head even when she's not around. It's like when a song gets stuck on mental replay, except it's a single note. Morgan's ummms are G3 below middle C. You could tune the whole choir to it. Morgan's a soprano like Ella, or like Ella *used* to be because Morgan refuses to sing harmony to anyone else's melody. She's also an actress and dancer and brags about being a triple threat. I agree that she's a triple threat but not in the way she wants everyone to think she is. Morgan has her envy-green eyes on something she constantly refers to as "global multiplatform domi-nation." Knowing Morgan, she'll get it. Morgan always gets what she wants. This is why Morgan is Ella's best friend and duet partner and not me.

My parents totally disapprove of Morgan's and Ella's parents for giving permission to post videos across all the socials. Mom says too many clients end up in her office because they believe they'll be rich and famous, and never develop any employable skills. Dad pushes me toward practical activities like FUNdamentals of Science. What's the point in putting so much time, energy, and money into music if I'm not destined for Juilliard? The only reason they ever approved of choir was because we rehearsed at school and they weren't inconvenienced by carpooling.

Neither parent noticed when they didn't get an invitation to last year's winter or spring concerts. I stayed home and the choir was no worse without me. Throughout sixth grade, from that ick-face day forward, I only pretended to sing. If Mrs. Mapleton were still there, she never would have let me get away with lip-synching. Mrs. Mapleton was the only person who encouraged me to sing loudly, proudly, beautifully. My former choir teacher was shorter than me, barely five feet tall in heels, but I looked up to her tremendously. She always dressed primly in pastel cardigans and full-skirted print dresses so everyone expected her to be a chirpy *trill-la-la-la* soprano. But she had a HUGE voice! A belty *ba-ba-ba-boom* alto that was all the more powerful because it came from such an unexpected source.

Maybe she saw—and heard—that same quality in me.

"What do you love about singing?" she asked me once after class.

"When I sing, it's like . . ." I hesitated, unsure of how to say it. "It's like . . . I'm letting out all the feelings I don't even know I have!"

Kaytee K. anthems made me feel powerful and fun. Riley Quick ballads made me feel swoony and romantic. I loved Broadway show tunes most of all because I could become anyone—a chatty meerkat, a misunderstood witch, a nineteenth-century French revolutionary—and escape my ordinary life for the duration of a song.

I didn't expect Mrs. Mapleton to understand what I was trying to say—that's why I preferred singing, after all—but she did.

"You sing to lose yourself and find yourself."

It was the most profound thing any adult has ever said to me. Before or since.

Mrs. Mapleton didn't come back for our sixth grade year. Her husband got a tenured job at a university in Portland, Oregon, which basically means he can never be fired. Dad says job security in higher education is hard to come by so they definitely made the right choice.

Mrs. Mapleton was replaced by a chirpy *trill-la-la-la* soprano straight out of choir college, who encouraged us to call her Miss Becky. Miss Becky had no idea I used to be a belty alto who tried out for every solo, sang in talent shows, and volunteered to organize sheet music after school. That girl was replaced by another who silently, sullenly moved her mouth along to the music.

I stopped singing. But MorganElla still called me Ickface.

POSITIVE CONTAGION

"SO ARE YOU A KAYTEE K. FAN?" KAYTEE ASKS. "ARE YOU A KAYTER?"

I don't pay much attention to either star. Mom prefers Riley Quick because her music is wholesome and positive, which is a refreshing break from all the unwholesome negativity she experiences every day as a social worker. Dad is an environmental scientist so he prefers Kaytee K. because she wrote "2 Hott N Herre" about global warming and "Oh Oh Ocean" about endangered sea life.

I'm trying to figure out just how much of this I want to tell Kaytee when she changes the subject again.

"What's under the plastic?"

"It's not plastic," I explain. "It's biodegradable wrap, better for the envi—"

She's always going on about the end of the planet in her know-it-all voice.

I stop myself. I try again.

"My mom wanted to bring them herself, but she's at work."

Most of this is true. The at-work part is. The wanted-to-bring-them-herself part not so much. For a social worker, Mom isn't very social. And my dad is even worse, especially when working on a book. As the daughter of two introverts, it's a miracle I ever leave my house. That's why Mom sends me on delivery missions, to encourage me to be more outgoing than I—and my parents—are by nature.

"We just got back from vacation . . ."

Kaytee peeks under the biodegradable wrap and sniffs.

"Bummer," she says. "I thought they were cupcakes."

She smiles as she says it. I smile in return. I like how Kaytee doesn't even pretend to care one bit about why my mom hadn't delivered the muffins herself. But that isn't the reason I'm grinning like a goofball at this girl I don't even know. I'm smiling because Kaytee's positivity is contagious.

And for the first time ever, I'm glad Mom forced me to be friendly.

AWKWARD ACQUAINTANCE MUFFINS

MOM ALWAYS MAKES ME DELIVER AWKWARD ACQUAINTANCE MUFFINS to neighbors she doesn't know very well who are going through major life events.

The funny thing about the Awkward Acquaintance Muffins is that they aren't even from a secret family recipe or anything. They're apple spice muffins from a mix you can buy pretty much at any supermarket with an organic foods aisle. My mom chops up a real apple and adds it to the mix to trick recipients of the Awkward Acquaintance Muffins into thinking that they're home-made. Awkward Acquaintance Muffins are for people she doesn't know well enough to make the muffins from scratch but wants them to think they are.

"So this kind of lying is okay?" I once asked.

She took off her glasses. Mom always does this when she needs a moment to consider how to answer my questions.

"It's lying," she said, "only if I bragged about them being homemade. It's not lying if they *assume* they're homemade."

"But you *want* them to think they're homemade," I said. "Or you wouldn't bother with the chopped apple."

She put her glasses back on.

"It makes the recipient feel special," she said. "No harm done."

"But Dad says a person's character is defined by our choices and—"

"Just deliver the muffins, Soph," she said wearily. "And if you want to clear your conscience by telling them that they came from a box, that's up to you."

The deception still felt wrong, but I went ahead and delivered the Awkward Acquaintance Muffins to the family up the street with the new baby. I didn't mention the mix. I didn't clear my conscience. Not then, or with the recovering-from-hip-surgery family on the corner, or with the wife-of-fifty-years-died family next door.

It felt less wrong every time. No harm done.

Before Kaytee's family moved in, the Delanos were our next-door neighbors my whole life. We weren't close and I won't miss them. They weren't awful people or anything, just old. If Mom and Dad wanted to hang out with old people, they'd make more of an effort to visit their own parents. All four live in Florida, though not together in the same condo or anything because that would be a bad sitcom situation, a boring show with zero viewers that gets canceled after the first season. Mom encouraged me to wave whenever we saw Mr. Delano in dress socks and New Balance sneakers cruising around the lawn on his riding mower. She reminded me to smile whenever we spotted Mrs. Delano in her purple velour tracksuit getting into her gas guzzler to drive thirty seconds to the grocery store visible from our front yards.

Nine months after delivering Awkward Acquaintance Muffins to the widowed Mr. Delano, I returned this morning to deliver another batch to the new family next door.

I won't clear my conscience with them either.

QUITTING WHILE AHEAD

KAYTEE PLANTS HER HANDS ON THE GRASS TO GO INTO ANOTHER handstand. She kicks her upturned legs back and forth just inches from my face.

"Sweet," I say.

And I immediately feel awkward because "sweet" is a word I say when I'm trying too hard.

She lands back on her feet.

"What's sweet?"

"What you were just doing," I say. "Walking on your hands like that."

She shrugs.

"No biggity," she says.

This time I recognize the Kaytee K. lyric right way. The next line is "Yo diggin' me?" and it annoys me every time I hear it. Even inside my own head. It's a fake rhyme. I hate fake rhymes but

I'm too distracted by my own cautious curiosity to get too annoyed about it right now. There's a question I want to ask Kaytee, but I'm too afraid to find out the answer. It's the question all incoming seventh graders have been asking one another since we got our welcome letters from Mercer Middle School earlier this month:

"What House are you?"

Mercer Middle School divides students into two Houses. We're assigned one or the other at random—it's not like the Dragonologist Chronicles, where the magical Cauldron of Serpentyne sorts clans by personality type. (FYI: I'm FlutterFluster, which makes sense because I don't really fit in anywhere.) House One is on the first floor, House Two is on the second floor, and lunch and gym are the only periods that mix us up.

I'm in House Two.

I don't know where MorganElla has been placed, and I'm too scared to find out. It could be a whole new start, or another year of the terrible same. If we're in different Houses, maybe MorganElla will target her evil attention on some other victim. But if we're in the same House, I'm a goner. Similarly, Kaytee's response could doom our friendship before it even gets a chance to begin. If she's in House One—with or without MorganElla—there's no way she'll choose me over more popular options. I'll be forced to spend the next six years of my life until college trying to avoid the enemy next door.

"Are you a gymnast?" I ask instead.

"Nope," she says. "But I love to dance."

She pirouettes to make her point.

"Sweet." I really need to stop saying the word "sweet."

"It's like a millionbilliontrillion degrees in New Jersey! And humid! Like I'm wearing a wet sweater!" Kaytee fans herself. "Do you want to come inside to cool off and see my room?"

Her sudden invitation takes me by surprise.

I do want to see her room.

But.

This conversation is going well.

Too well.

I need to say goodbye to Kaytee before I say something dumb.

I need to get out of here before she regrets the invitation.

"Maybe next time," I say.

Next time, I tell myself, I'll ask what I really want to know.

TO DOING

BUILDING A RAIN BARREL IS SAFER THAN VISITING KAYTEE'S ROOM.
This is number 76 in *The Book of Awesome for Awesome Girls* but
it's only the twenty-ninth I've completed so far because I'm not To
Doing them in numerical order.

I choose my To Dos based on how much time is required to
complete them. The longer it takes, the better. The ideal project
requires between one and two hours to gather supplies, another
one to two hours for reading and comprehending the instructions,
followed by four to six hours of assembly. If I schedule enough
breaks, the very best projects can stretch out over two or three
days. It's a tough balance though, because if I take *too many* breaks,
brainchatter fills the void by thinking too much about how Ella is
spending her first summer without me.

From start to finish, I estimate building the rain barrel will
take me about eight hours. I could probably stretch it out over

another day or two, but meeting Kaytee this morning motivates me to get it done in one.

First, I have to walk to the hardware store to purchase my materials: a clean trash can with lid, a spigot, a hose clamp, an assortment of rubber and metal washers, and Teflon tape. If the owners think it's strange that their newest and most loyal customer is an almost twelve-year-old girl who always pays in cash, they haven't let on. Fortunately, the hardware store is very close to our house on the boring side of Stockton Square, far enough away from Frootie Smoothie and Urban Outfitters and the Mercer Community Pool that I don't have to worry about being seen hauling home my supplies. I'm a little concerned about being caught by Kaytee, but she's nowhere in sight when I drag my purchases up the driveway. (Two hours.)

Next, I read and reread the step-by-step instructions provided by the Awesome Girls Team. Just to reinforce that knowledge and—okay, kill some more time—I watch the highest-rated YouTube tutorials on well-reviewed home and garden channels. (Two and a half hours.)

Then I get to work. I use a power drill to bore a hole near the bottom of the can. I install, seal, and secure the spigot with a hose clamp. I use a precision knife to cut holes into the lid for water to flow in and pour out. I set it on a platform of bricks under the downspout. This straightforward description makes the process sound a lot easier than it really was. (Four hours.)

Finally, I look at what I've accomplished.

According to the Awesome Girls Team, here's what I should be thinking:

Woo-hoo! I used my brain and my own two hands to construct a rain-collection system I can use to water indoor and outdoor plants. I'm helping the environment by cutting back on water usage and reducing harmful runoff into lakes, streams, and rivers. Most important, I'm showing the world that girls aren't afraid to get their hands dirty and pick up a power tool or two!

But here's what I'm really thinking:

Eight and one-half hours down.

I made it through another lonely day.

A PROMISE

MOM GETS HOME FROM WORK IN TIME FOR THE THREE OF US TO SIT down to dinner. She struggles with leaving her caseloads behind at the office and tonight is no exception. I've just cut my veggie burger in half when Mom starts the night's discussion with "Remember the pregnant teen . . . ?"

Lately my mom has been worrying about a sixteen-year-old in her third trimester who was kicked out of her house and has nowhere to live. That's the kind of social worker she is. When Mom talks about clients, she communicates in bullet points to protect their privacy.

"Parents out of the picture."

Mom taps out bullet point number one on the table with a spoon.

"Lived with the boyfriend."

Tap.

"Picked up for selling drugs."

Tap.

"Smart girl."

Tap.

"Could do so much with her life if only given the opportunity."

Tap, tap.

Adults are surprised by the conversations my parents have in front of me. Not a lot of almost twelve-year-olds chat about teen pregnancy and drug dealers at dinner. It's normal kale salad conversation around here. I can handle it, though I do more listening than talking. Sometimes I wonder if they open up around me because they've forgotten I'm there.

Anyway, it turns out that the sixteen-year-old's troubles are just beginning because she tested positive for marijuana, which is not only bad for the baby she's growing inside her but is also a violation of her probation, and well, you get the idea. The whole situation is just awful and I lose count of the bullet points Mom taps out with her kale salad fork after she hits number nine.

Eventually Mom asks Dad about the progress of his book, which is based on research he's conducted at the university lab for the past five years or so. The working title is *Extreme Precipitation: The Dry Gets Drier and the Wet Gets Wetter* and I'm sure he can make it more interesting than it sounds. He's on sabbatical, which is just a fancy professor way of saying he's on a break to write his book. I'd offer to finish it for him myself if it meant I could take my own sabbatical from middle school.

When the book is done, Dad is supposed to go back to teaching. He reminds Mom how he never wants to return to the classroom because kids today only care about getting good grades. They aren't interested in learning.

"Sophie!" It is the first time he's addressed me the entire meal. "Knowledge is the reward for hard work."

"Got it." I nod. "Knowledge is the reward for hard work."

Mom puts down her fork and tilts her head at me with interest. I take advantage of the moment.

"Like today I learned how to make a rain barrel out of a trash can. It took me all day but I stuck to it until I crossed it off my To Do List."

My parents give each other looks like *Hmm . . . maybe that book isn't so bad after all.*

The Book of Awesome for Awesome Girls is the kind of book adults give girls my age to curb our addiction to screens and social media and technology. I'm probably the only girl in the world who was so lonely and desperate that I walked to our local bookstore and used my straight-A report card money to buy it for myself behind my parents' backs. You'd think they'd be all for it, but they don't like books, toys, clothes, or *anything* that's supergirlie or superboyish because they send the message that boys and girls must live by different sets of rules. Girls are as capable as boys, but we lack confidence. And the confidence gap between girls and boys starts when we're babies and just expands wider and wider and wider as we get older, and Dad says that's why there are twice as many men than women in the environmental sciences program at the university.

Worse, Mom says too many girls end up in her office because they dumbed themselves down to fit ditzy female stereotypes.

Yes, my parents really talk to me like this.

I didn't want to tell them about the book, but it's way harder to be sneaky with a thick hardcover than it is with a skinny phone. My parents "caught" me with it as soon as I returned from the bookstore. And while they still disapprove of its title and hot pink cover, they've decided that its overall Can Do message is a mostly positive one.

And maybe the book will surprise me. Maybe it will turn out to be so much more than 100 Ways to Fill My Empty Days. Maybe I'll discover that I've got a green thumb (number 74: "Plant a Vegetable Garden") or a world traveler's tongue (number 22: "Learn to Say 'Thank You' in a Dozen Languages"). Maybe finding a new passion will put enough distance between me and my abandoned passion that I'll be able to come back to it just long enough to pull off Impossible Number 45, which I didn't know was a To Do until I'd already committed myself to the book. So far, it hasn't panned out like that. I haven't found a replacement passion. Not yet anyway.

Impossible Number 45 looms.

If it were last summer, Ella and I could do number 45 together.

If it were last summer, Impossible Number 45 wouldn't be impossible.

If it were last summer, I wouldn't need a To Do List to fill my empty days.

"I also met the new girl today," I say while I still have my parents' attention. "Like you told me to, Mom."

"Oh! You did?"

Mom says it like she's forgotten all about forcing me to go over there this morning.

"So tell me, Sophie. What kind of people constructed this architectural monstrosity that's as ugly as it is irresponsible?"

The Rays tore down the Delanos' tiny ranch and built a much bigger vinyl-sided box with lots of energy-inefficient windows. They paid tons of money, more than any other house on our street. Mom says it's good for the neighborhood. Dad says it's bad for the planet. He doesn't like it when rich people cut down trees to build too-big houses.

"Their daughter seems nice, Dad," I say. "Her name is Kaytee. Like the singer. Kaytee K.?"

My father is unimpressed.

"Kaytee K.," my mom repeats. "Which one is she again?"

"She's the biggest female pop star who isn't Riley Quick," I say.

"The mermaid?" Mom guesses.

"Right."

Mom taps her fork like she's pleased for figuring it out.

"Did they like the muffins?" she asks.

Dad clears his throat but doesn't say anything. He doesn't have to. He's said many times that Mom is too emotionally invested in muffins that come out of a box.

"I don't know. I'll find out tomorrow."

I say it out loud to make it official. Promises made inside my head are too easy to break.

DÉJÀ VU

I HOPE KAYTEE WILL BE IN THE FRONT YARD AGAIN. BUT I'M PRETTY much expecting her not to be. For the first time in a long time, hope wins out! Kaytee *is* out there, walking on her hands just like yesterday! Except for today's orange and gray tank tops, it's the same scene as the day before. Like the best kind of déjà vu.

Unfortunately my optimism is fleeting.

I'm headed in Kaytee's direction when a shiny luxury SUV slowly passes in front of my house. I catch flashes of flame-red and honey-blonde ponytails in the back window and I'm overtaken by the terrifying realization that MorganElla has been spying on me this whole time! The girlbeast is here to warn Kaytee not to say another word to me, rescuing her from the humiliation of accidentally befriending Mercer Middle School's biggest loser-to-be . . .

Woof! Woof! Woof!

The sound is muffled but unmistakable. Those aren't pony-tails, but *dog* tails. I've mistaken MorganElla for an Irish setter and a golden retriever. If my heart weren't palpitating, I might even laugh at my paranoia.

Kaytee springs to her feet when she sees me on the grass.

"Hey!"

I've barely recovered from my fright. I try to disguise the tremble in my voice.

"H-hey!"

She looks me up and down for a few seconds.

"I have to ask," Kaytee says.

I brace myself for the worst. She doesn't need MorganElla to sound the loser alarm. She sees through my facade right down to the Ickface I really am.

"Is your shirt Eco/Echo? Not the button-down, but the red-and-yellow one underneath?"

I nod slowly.

"I recognized the signature swirly design from this month's *Teen Vogue*! They're one of 'Five Brands Making the World a Better Place.'"

I didn't know that. I've always had sensitive skin, but in sixth grade I started getting itchy rashes all over my body. I think it was stress related, but my parents blamed hormones. Normal girls get a few pimples during puberty. I got allergic contact dermatitis. My parents started buying this superorganic brand because it uses all-natural fabrics and low-impact dyes that don't cause hives. Bonus:

Everything in the Eco/Echo line matches everything else and I don't waste brainpower anymore worrying about whether my Dragonologist Chronicles FLUTTERFYRE FOR PRESIDENT shirt is as babyish as MorganElla said it was.

"So faboosh," Kaytee says.

I feel myself blushing. No one compliments my clothes. Then, without warning, Kaytee pulls at the corner of my shirt and knots it at the hip just like hers. She takes a step backward and fans out her hands.

"Even faboosher!"

"Thank you!"

"You're welcome. Come up and see my room!"

And before I can say yes or no, Kaytee tips herself upside down again.

"Get the door for me?"

Kaytee doesn't teeter one bit as she leads me through the Rays' front entrance. Jumbo unopened moving boxes line the walls and Kaytee confidently navigates her way through the narrowed hall on her hands. This house is bigger than the Delanos' ranch but doesn't feel all that much bigger than our own. I'm having trouble taking in all the dimensions and details though, because I'm too distracted by the most gorgeous grand piano I've ever seen outside a concert hall! It's in the middle of a mostly empty room next to the kitchen and I'm drawn to it like a dumb moth to our front porch light. My finger is a half inch away from pressing the lowest note when Kaytee breaks the spell.

"Follow me," Kaytee says, still upside down. "This way."

I'm still thinking about the piano as I follow her down the hall. I'm expecting to be greeted by Kaytee's mother at any moment. Where is she anyway? And her father for that matter. Are they home? They have to be home, right? They wouldn't leave Kaytee alone in this new house in a town where she doesn't know anyone and is bored and lonely and could get into a lot of trouble, would they? Mom says too many clients end up in her office because of bad decisions made out of boredom.

But then I spot a boy sitting on the far end of an L-shaped leather sectional, plugged in so he can't hear us. He looks like he's our age, but it's hard to tell because he's sitting down and I'm not the best judge of such things. MorganElla could size him up and guess his date of birth down to the minute.

Kaytee flips back onto her feet.

"Ignore him."

She screws up her face and before I know what I'm doing or why, I make the *ew* face too.

"My brother, Lexi," she explains as we go up the stairs. "He's supposed to be working on his summer school assignments, but I know he's watching FIFA training videos on YouTube because he's *obsessed* with playing A-team soccer this fall."

Kaytee flicks her hand in a fancy way when she says "obsessed." All her gestures are intentional and funny. If they were unintentional, like an Ickface tic, they might still be funny but in a mean way.

"Wilson Academy is supposed to be way better for Lexi because he needs more discipline and, like, academic attention and stuff," she says. "My dad went there and he turned out to be a responsible adult and all but still, I don't buy it. You put a bunch of ten- to fourteen-year-old boys together in a building and the combination of old farts and new hormones does something to their brains to make them all"—she holds up imaginary attack claws—"*Grrrrrr*."

I'm supposed to laugh, but I'm thinking too much about what happens when you put a bunch of ten- to fourteen-year-old girls together in one room. Then all of a sudden it hits me: Maybe I won't have to worry about Kaytee's answer to the House question after all.

"Are you going to private school too?"

I'm not sure what answer I want to hear. If Kaytee says no, then there's a chance for us to be House Two Besties at Mercer Middle School . . . but also the possibility of a House One bond-a-thon with MorganElla. If she says yes, then at least I know she's safe from MorganElla . . . while also guaranteeing another lonely year for me. Neither option is all good or all bad.

"Ugh, yes," Kaytee says, ending my suspense.

I try not to look too relieved. Or disappointed. Because I'm a little bit of both at the same time.

"Why *ugh*?" I ask.

"I'm too much of a free spirit."

And then she does this silly hula dance to illustrate her free spiritedness.

I wonder what private school she's going to? I know a lot about private schools around here. I've done my research. I excel at research. Kaytee asks her next question before I get a chance to ask mine.

"Are you ready for total fabooshness?"

I'm not sure I am, but I say yes anyway.

LOSER DOLPHIN

UNLIKE THE REST OF THE HOUSE. KAYTEE'S ROOM IS PERFECTLY PUT together, like she's lived here for years. It's twice the size of mine and, yes, totally faboosh. There's a glitzy chandelier, dramatic floor-to-ceiling curtains, piles of blinged-out pillows, fluffy floor poufs, a movie-star makeup mirror, plus an entire wall devoted to scarves and hats and belts and necklaces and more accessories than I've ever seen outside the drama department costume closet.

"Tell the truth," Kaytee says, her shoulders squared, hands on hips. "Are these walls bluish-green or greenish-blue?"

I consider the question before asking one of my own.

"Which one means more green than blue?"

"Aha! More green than blue! That's what I hoped you'd say!" Kaytee claps with joy. "This paint color is the closest I could get to match Kaytee K.'s fins!"

She points to a framed poster of Kaytee K. hanging in a

can't-miss spot right above the bed. She's dressed in her famous mermaid costume, the one she wore all the time when her song "Oh Oh Ocean" was popular. The wall color really does match the shimmery mermaid scales in the poster.

"We had it painted twice to get it right. The first time it came out way too dark blue and I hated it. Then we tried this greener aquamarine shade and whoop! Success!"

As she speaks, I notice subtle patterns all over the walls. They're painted just the teensiest bit darker than the main wall color. Or maybe these patterns are the same color, only shinier . . . ?

"Oooh! You'll love this!" Kaytee promises.

"Love what?"

"Back up. Take in the whole wall at once."

I do as instructed. I'm ready to tell her that I don't see anything when all of a sudden I see what I didn't know I was looking for!

"Whoa!"

"Yessss!" Kaytee claps again. "You spotted them!"

"Dolphins!"

And it isn't the same dolphin stenciled on the wall over and over again. One dives, another floats on its back, yet another appears to be treading water in circles. A whole pod.

"Dolphins are second only to humans in intelligence," Kaytee says.

I know that. But sometimes it's good to let people think they're teaching you something.

"Really?" I ask.

"They're sophisticated, like, *emotionally* too," Kaytee goes on. "Dolphins make best friends and even have cliques!"

I did not know this.

"Really?" I ask for real this time.

"Really! They'll shun loser dolphins who don't belong!"

I try to figure out which loser dolphin is the Ickface of the group. Until I remember the loser Ickface dolphin wouldn't be welcome on the wall at all.

Kaytee juts her chin at me, wanting some kind of response.

"I love the dolphins."

My parents might approve of the dolphins and the greenish-blue wall color, but probably not the Kaytee K. poster. *Definitely* not the chandelier, floor poufs, or pile of blingy pillows.

My parents decorated my nursery in black and white because sharp visual contrast is best for infant stimulation. They also liked that it wasn't stereotypically girlish or boyish, so they stuck with it as I got older. Thanks to my parents, my wall color hasn't warped my young mind into thinking I can't be a scientist. I'm not sure if I *want* to be a scientist, but that's a different problem.

"You really don't think it's weird to have dolphins on my walls?" Kaytee asks.

"No," I assure her. "I think it's cool."

Kaytee doesn't reply. She just traces a finger along a dorsal fin, as if she were under the spell of her own walls. If it were possible to dive into those painted waters, would she jump right in to join their deep-sea clique?

I understand wanting to disappear. I really do.

I also understand wanting to be noticed.

Even with only a few days left of summer, I hope the walls mean Kaytee is the type of girl who prefers the open ocean to public pools.

I didn't always hate the pool.

Mercer Community Pool isn't an evil place. It's not haunted by the ghost of a boy who dove skull-first into the shallow end or anything. The whole pool complex was overhauled in a major renovation a few years ago. There are actually four different pools: a wading pool for toddlers, a lap pool for serious swimmers, a dive pool for show-offy teens trying to outdo one another, and a play pool for the rest of us.

Until this summer, Ella and I would spend hours in the play pool trying to see how much "play" the lifeguards would let us get away with. Ella would climb up on my shoulders to challenge Harumi and Sofie-with-an-F in chicken fights, or we'd splash around with our eyes shut, shouting, "MARCO!!! POLO!!! MARCO!!! POLO!!!" When it was just the two of us, Ella and I entertained ourselves with our favorite game of all. Underwater karaoke was Ella's invention and the rules were simple: We'd both drop below the water's surface and one of us would sing a few lines of a popular song while the other guessed what it was. I came up choking the first few times we played, but I got really good at it—even better than Ella—once I mastered breathing out, not in! When we got too waterlogged, we'd towel off, buy snacks, and swap worn-out and re-re-reread copies of *The Dragonologist Chronicles* in the shade until it was time to go home. Ella loved these afternoons so much she'd often break into Riley Quick's fizziest pop tribute to the season and didn't care who heard her.

She'd sing, *"Summer bliss, summer bliss."*

I'd join in, *"We will never forget this."*

We'd sing together, *"Summer bliss, summer bliss. We will never forget this."*

Underwater and on land, Ella lied.

Now it's all about being seen—about making the scene. MorganElla says it's crucial to hang out at the pool the summer before seventh grade because it's the best way to practice being popular in middle school. If you rock it half naked at the pool, you can rock it fully dressed at school.

"Confidence," MorganElla likes to say, "is way intimidating."

Leave it to MorganElla to turn self-esteem into a weapon.

None of this stuff comes easy to me. I can't fake excitement about the things all girls are supposed to love. I get bored talking about boys. I can't name any beauty gurus and don't watch makeup or hair tutorials. I haven't figured out how to pose for flattering selfies and will never be "aesthetic." My parents won't let me have my own phone or sign up for any social media, but I secretly don't mind because the pressure to keep up appearances on all the socials would be way too much for me to handle anyway.

Until sixth grade, I would've said the same exact thing about Ella. I honestly don't know when these skills started mattering to her, or how she so easily mastered them once they did. Is there a secret list of To Dos that only the right kind of girls have access to? Ella went through a phase when she was obsessed with the Illuminati, the mysterious group of superpowerful celebrities who allegedly rule the world. (Both Riley Quick and Kaytee K. are rumored to be members.) I never bought into Ella's conspiracy theories before, but if she ever reveals her membership in the Global Middle School Illuminati, I won't be shocked. And if it *does* exist, there's no doubt Kaytee will get her invitation soon if she hasn't already.

For all these reasons and many more, going to two different schools is the best possible thing that could happen for me and Kaytee. The New Girl will never need to find out what an Ickface I really am.

"You won't tell anyone I'm, like, a weirdo obsessed with marine life, or anything?" Kaytee asks. "Will you?"

I swear I wouldn't ever say anything like that about her. I leave out that I have no one to tell.

If Kaytee went to Mercer, MorganElla would probably find out even without my help. MorganElla has shady ways of getting information, maybe via the Global Middle School Illuminati? And if it's even the tiniest bit embarrassing, the girlbeast never, ever lets you hear the end of it either. She'd give Kaytee an innocent-sounding nickname, the kind of nickname that could get around our school's anti-bullying policy, because MorganElla is an evil genius when it comes to finding ways around our school's anti-bullying policy. Even when her nicknames aren't so innocent—like Ickface, Chewy, or Lickity Lick—she *still* doesn't get in trouble for using them.

Anyway, it would be classic MorganElla for her to call Kaytee "Flipper," which she'd get away with because it's the name of a dolphin from an ancient TV show only my Dad remembers because he really *is* a weirdo obsessed with marine life. And then Maddy and everyone else would call her Flipper too. And maybe Flipper wouldn't be too bad at first, not as obviously bad as Ickface, Chewy, or Lickity Lick, but it would get irritating when MorganElla refused to trade it in for Kaytee's real name.

"Are you sure it isn't too blue in here?"

The more Kaytee asks, the more I start to doubt my own eyes. I stick with my original answer.

"Definitely more green than blue," I say. "It's oceanic."

"Oceanic," Kaytee repeats. "I like that. Like 'Oh Oh Ocean.'"

Exactly, I think.

Kaytee bounces over to her desk and removes a hot pink Magic Marker from its package.

"Do you ever practice your signature?" she asks. "You know, in case you get famous?"

I shake my head. I can't think of a single reason why I would ever be famous enough for anyone to want my autograph. Not anymore anyway.

"My brother says celebrities don't even get asked for autographs anymore because it's all about selfies."

Ella would agree with him on that. She bragged about posting five hundred selfies, which I guess was a sixth grade record. And that was back in late June, so she'll probably double that number by the time we start Mercer Middle the day after tomorrow. Who knows? If I were as pretty as Ella, maybe I'd take pictures of myself making duckface in my tiny bikini too.

"I like practicing anyway. K-A-Y-T-E-E." She pantomimes writing each letter in the air. "And I always punctuate my signature with a little happy face or a sad face or mad face, depending on my mood."

"Like an emoji?"

"Yesssss!"

I think she's giving me the marker to practice my signature, so I'm surprised when she firmly clasps my hand and flips it over to the backside. Kaytee uncaps the marker with her teeth and autographs the back of my hand in hot pink, swirly cursive.

An exclamation point is dotted with a happy face!

"You're happy?"

Kaytee doesn't answer right away. She's too busy taking a great big sniff of the bubble-gum-scented marker. She's about to stick it back in the cap still clenched in her teeth when she pauses to offer me a whiff of my own. First her lip gloss, now her marker. Kaytee is a sharer. The way she presents it reminds me of the once-a-year parties for Dad's university colleagues when I get all dressed up to serve hors d'oeuvres and impress everyone with how mature I am for my age. *Would you care for a crab cake? A meatball? Bubble gum Magic Marker?*

"No thanks," I say.

Marker sniffing can be a serious addiction. Not enough parents warn their almost twelve-year-olds about all the sneaky killers in the craft store. Countless lives have been ruined by huffing markers, paint remover, and glue. Is Kaytee in a happy mood because she's loopy from the brain-scrambling chemicals in the marker? Her brother is too busy YouTubing to take responsibility for his sister's actions. It's my obligation to find out.

"So why are you happy?" I ask.

"Why am I happy?" She dances around in a circle, swishing her ponytail to and fro. "I'm happy because I've made my first friend in New Jersey!"

Between yesterday and today, we've known each other for no more than ten minutes. And yet, I already feel like I know her better than anyone from Shadybrook Elementary.

I should probably leave before I say or do something wrong.

I should probably go home to work on a To Do.

But I don't.

I stay.

LIKE MOTHER, LIKE DAUGHTER

KAYTEE'S MOM COMES HOME SHORTLY AFTER SHE CAPS THE PINK marker. She's wearing heels and a navy dress that wraps around her slim waist. It's a professional look but it's only mid-morning, so I doubt Mrs. Ray is returning from the office.

"I never leave the kids on their own like this!" she insists.

She wants me to know that it is *not* okay that Kaytee invited me over unsupervised and without parental approval. Mrs. Ray seems concerned with my first impression of her. I think she's afraid I'll report her neglectful parenting to the authorities.

"Kaytee! What have I told you about having friends over when I'm out?"

"Sophie's our neighbor, Mom," she says. "Neighbors invite each other over."

"But not when I'm out of the house!" She turns to me. "Our new babysitter canceled at the last minute . . ."

"Moooooooooom," Kaytee whines. "Girls my age don't need *baby*sitters. Girls my age *are* babysitters. In fact . . ." She swivels her neck in a sassy way. "You should pay me for babysitting Lexi all morning." She rolls her shoulders. "Money." Shoulder roll. "Money." Shoulder roll. "Money." Shoulder roll.

Mrs. Ray tries to keep a straight face to maintain her dignity as an authority figure, but she just can't do it. Her daughter is irrepressible.

"You," she says, tugging on Kaytee's ponytail.

"Me," Kaytee replies, fluttering her eyelashes.

"I'm glad you liked the muffins I brought yesterday," I say, pointing at the plate on the counter.

Our welcome gift looks like it was attacked by a starving bear that just woke up from hibernation. The biodegradable wrapping has been torn off and thrown carelessly to the floor. Of the dozen muffins I delivered, three and a half remain. Plus crumbs.

Kaytee forgets all about the cupcakes she really wanted.

"Lexi! You ate all the muffins!"

The boy from the couch saunters into the kitchen swinging a gallon of milk.

"I told you to stop calling me that," he says.

"Oh my god, *Alex*. You ate all the muffins! Mom told you to save some for me!"

"You're exaggerating." He tips his head back and chugs straight from the jug. "I ate eight." He wipes a milk mustache with the back of his hand. "And a half."

I remind myself not to drink milk at the Rays' house.

"Alexander Michael Ray!" Mrs. Ray says sharply. "Sophie will think you don't have any manners."

"Who's Sophie?"

I told you. Boys don't notice me *at all*. This is fine by me because it seems like everything changes when boys start noticing you. Last summer Ella raced me to be the first one off the high dive. We didn't want the lifeguards to blow the whistle at us for breaking the "No Running" rule on the concrete pool deck, so we'd speedwalked really, really fast and Ella stuck out her elbows and pumped her arms in this silly way that made me laugh and . . .

Well.

Now Ella takes long, slow laps *around* the pool but never *in* it.

Now Ella wants the lifeguard to blow the whistle at her because he's "cute."

Now Ella would sooner delete a thousand selfies than ever agree to look silly in public on purpose.

"Hi, Alex," I say, making sure to use his preferred name. "I'm Sophie. I live next door."

He replies with a burp, then laughs like a madman.

Mrs. Ray hides her face in her hands. Kaytee gives him a great shove.

"Is that what they're teaching you at summer school?" Mrs. Ray says into her hands. "Belching?"

"Of course not, Mom," Alex replies with a grin. "Wilson men are also taught the art of the fart."

And then—ohnoooo!—he lets one rip! I swear Mrs. Ray is

about to faint with mortification. Alex from laughter. Kaytee from the smell. She frantically fans the air as Alex takes the stairs two at a time, laughing like a maniac the whole way.

"I apologize for my son," Mrs. Ray says. "He's . . ."

She struggles to find the right word. Kaytee supplies it as she grabs a can from under the sink.

"Gross!"

Air freshener chemicals are far worse for our health than Alex's foul-smelling flatulence, or fragrant markers for that matter. But Kaytee is determined to shower the kitchen in rose-scented poison and there's no way to stop her. If Dad were here, he wouldn't need to wait for the slow, painful death from inhaling too many toxins. He would have a heart attack right on the spot. He has similarly strong feelings about dryer sheets, microbeads in antibacterial soaps, and turtleneck sweaters. The last one doesn't have anything to do with the environment. He just doesn't like turtleneck sweaters.

"Speaking of schools," Mrs. Ray says, steering the conversation back to where she wants it. "I just had a lovely sit-down with the headmaster of Villa Academy, Kaytee."

"Villa Academy!" I blurt out. "You're going to Villa Academy?"

Kaytee shrugs.

"Are you familiar with Villa Academy?" Mrs. Ray asks.

Am I familiar? I know everything about it! It's a tiny all-girls school with a superstrict admissions policy. It never accepts more than ten girls in the *entire grade*. That's one-tenth of what I can expect at Mercer Middle. Based on those numbers, I figure the odds of having a girlbeast as awful as MorganElla at Villa Academy are very, very small. On the flip side, if there were a girlbeast as awful as MorganElla at Villa Academy, there'd be nowhere to hide.

Not that hiding has done me much good.

None of this matters because my parents won't let me apply to Villa, Ivy, Stuart, Lawrenceville, Hun, or any of the other local private schools I researched as part of my escape plan. Mom and Dad are against private schools because they're exclusive *and* expensive. At Mercer Middle School, lessons in exclusivity will come free of charge.

I realize Mrs. Ray is still waiting for an answer to her question. The subject of Villa Academy revs up tummyrumble big-time but I try to remain calm in my response.

"Yes, I know it," I finally reply. "It's got a great STEM program."

"Stem program?" Kaytee crosses her eyes, flares her nostrils. "Like flowers? I like flowers. Flowers are sooooooooo purrrrrrrty. And they smelllllll sooooooo goooooooood." She sprays more air freshener above her head.

"Science, technology, engineering, and math," Mrs. Ray explains, cracking a smile at her daughter's antics despite her best efforts not to. "Please continue, Sophie."

Kaytee isn't having it.

"OH MY GOD, MOM, THIS CONVERSATION IS SO BORING!"

Kaytee is tugging at the knot in my shirt like *Let's go*. And that is fine with me because I don't want to talk anymore about Villa Academy. Kaytee has no idea how lucky she is. I wish more than anything I could transfer to Villa Academy. I thought my parents might be persuaded by the STEM program's reputation, but I was wrong. I don't want to get into all that, but I can tell from Mrs. Ray's animated expression that for her this school conversation is just getting started. She is all lit up, just like Kaytee when she talked about dolphins or Kaytee K. In fact, once I see the mother-daughter resemblance, I can't unsee it. It's uncanny.

"Wow," I say. "You two are total look-alikes."

"Duhhhh! Of course Lexi—I mean *Alex*—and I are look-alikes!" Kaytee says. "We're twins!"

She and Alex are twins? I hadn't noticed a similarity—not any more or less than regular nonidentical siblings anyway—and I assumed he was a year or two older. Maybe my powers of observation were numbed in Alex's killer gas attack.

"I'm not talking about you and your brother," I reply.

"Huh?" Kaytee searches the room.

"You and your mom," I say.

It's obvious: petite but powerful, honey hair, tan skin, lively brown eyes.

Kaytee opens her mouth to speak, but nothing comes out. She must be so beyond mortified to be compared to her mom. She probably thinks Mrs. Ray is a total nerdball and is just about the last person on earth she'd ever want to look like. I feel that way about my own mom when she wears socks with Crocs.

Kaytee looks like she's about to cry and it's all my fault. Then Mrs. Ray puts her arm around her daughter's shoulder and Kaytee's face softens. She doesn't look teary anymore. She looks like herself again.

"Like mother, like daughter," Kaytee says. "But I wish I were even more like my mom on the inside."

PRACTICAL VS. EMOTIONAL

I DON'T WAIT FOR MY PARENTS TO ASK ME ABOUT THE NEW NEIGHBORS at dinner tonight.

"Mrs. Ray told me to thank you for the muffins," I say, "and you're welcome to drop by anytime but to excuse the mess because they're not moved in yet."

"You can drop by anytime because she's a stay-at-home mom," Dad says dryly, spiking a cherry tomato with his fork. "And surprise! Surprise! The father is in finance."

My dad dislikes the finance dads because "they benefit from a corrupt system that enables the richest one percent of Americans to amass more money than the bottom ninety percent." That is a direct quote, no exaggeration. Dad has repeated it countless times. It's like a ritual recitation in our house, the way other families say grace. I'm less clear on what Dad has against stay-at-home moms. It has something to do with wasted college educations and women making eighty cents on the dollar, but I don't hear that lecture as often as the one percent/ninety percent rant. Sometimes I wonder why he works so hard to save the earth when he dislikes most of the people who populate it. It's hard to keep track of all the reasons my dad has for disliking people and today I'm not in the mood to keep up.

My mother shoots him a look that says, *Stop it.*

Dad shoots her a look right back that says, *Who, me?*

"Let's keep it positive, shall we? There's way too much negativity in my life."

I'm with Mom on this one. I don't want to play along with Dad right now. First of all, the Rays' new construction isn't *that* much bigger than other houses on our block. Kaytee's mom mentioned something about it being owned by the company Kaytee's dad works for, so it's not like they designed it or even picked it out. And it's a shack compared with the humongous mansions in Morgan Middleton's neighborhood. She lives in the richest part of town, where its not uncommon for a house to include a movie theater or full-sized basketball court. Plus Kaytee and her mom were so nice to me all morning. Alex ignored me but he's an eleven-year-old boy so that's to be expected. I'm not the kind of eleven-year-old girl eleven-year-old boys pay any attention to. I can already tell that Kaytee *is* that kind of girl: pretty but not prissy. Ella used to be that way too.

"So do you like her, the new girl . . . ?"

Mom searches for her name.

"Kaytee," I tell her.

"Kaytee," she repeats.

My mom easily remembers the names and nicknames of every troubled youth who has passed through her office for the past decade and yet struggles to recall the names of any of my friends. And I can't blame her, really, when Ella was the only one I spent any major time with. I'll have to mention Kaytee's name a hundred more times before it gets fixed in Mom's brain.

"Yeah, I like *Kaytee* a lot," I say. "I'm thinking of spending tomorrow with *Kaytee*. Maybe *Kaytee* and I can make friendship bracelets."

Three *Kaytees* down, ninety-seven to go.

"Mmm," Mom says distractedly. "That sounds nice."

She's already thinking about how much better her clients' lives would be if they had wholesome besties for innocent fun like making friendship bracelets.

"Tomorrow is the last day of summer vacation," Dad says. "Isn't there a better way to prepare for your first year of middle school than making silly jewelry?"

I'm sure there are lots of better ways. If I were allowed, I could take Dad on a tour of all the socials and let him see for himself all the better ways awesomely well-adjusted about-to-be seventh graders are spending their last days of summer vacation.

"Surely that book of yours has more constructive To Dos," Dad says, raising his skeptical eyebrows.

"Oh, let her have her fun," Mom says. "Too many clients end up in my office because they suffer acute stress from hypercompetitive academic résumé building."

Then my parents get into a debate about encouraging practical versus emotional intelligence.

Kaytee and I haven't made plans to get together again. I know I'll see her eventually because we live right next door to each other but I hope it's sooner than later. I don't want to spend the last day of summer vacation as I've spent so many before.

Alone.

SIGNS

I'M WATCHING KAYTEE AND ALEX IN THEIR FRONT YARD FROM MY bedroom. They're passing a soccer ball back and forth, not just kicking, but bouncing off their knees and heads, whatever it takes to keep it in the air. I'm feeling a little weird about the open-endedness of our non-invitation to each other. *Will Kaytee think it's weird if I invite myself over to her house three days in a row? Will she figure out I have nowhere else to go on the last day of summer? Will she finally realize all on her own, without any help from MorganElla, what an Ickface I really am?*

Kaytee sends the ball flying with a whip-flip of her foot, too fast for Alex to get to it before it hits the ground. She pumps her fist in triumph. He punches her in the arm, picks up the ball, and skulks into the house without her. Kaytee looks up at my window and welcomes me over with a wave.

Did she know I was there the whole time? Does it matter?

I'm greeting her thirty seconds later.

"Hey," I say.

"Hey," Kaytee says back. "What are we up to today?"

We. Hooray! I feel silly for worrying all morning that my research would be for nothing.

"I looked up our birthdays," I say. "Want to hear something funny?"

"Sure."

"We're only a day apart but we have different signs."

"Signs?"

"Astrological signs," I explain. "You know. The zodiac. Horoscopes."

Number 26: "Research Your Zodiac Sign." I knew it wouldn't be a very good To Do. No supplies or assembly required, just research. I can stretch even the simplest To Dos into all-dayers (see number 21: "Research Another Awesome Girl with Your Same Name"), but this was a challenging topic for me.

Ella read her horoscope every day. For many years she wouldn't even eat breakfast until she'd consulted Sydney Stargazer's column in the newspaper. When she slept over at my house, even Mom knew to have it spread out next to her bowl of muesli. In fifth grade she got obsessed with an online astrologer calling herself Miss Z.

"Oooh! Today someone will have an impact on my life. I should start a new project or complete an old project. It's a perfect time to make big changes!"

I remember her grinning at her phone. We were sitting at the small round table I'd sat at hundreds, no, thousands, of times before. I sat in my usual spot, where a natural knot in the wood grain resembled a big-eyed space alien Ella called Ed. Ella sat across from me in her usual spot, at a plastic place mat printed with sunflowers. It hid the hole Ella had gouged into the table with her stabby pencil during a superfrustrating spelling test study session.

That was my last sleepover at her house, but I had no way of knowing at the time. If I *had* known, maybe I wouldn't have tried so hard to convince Ella her beloved horoscope was pseudoscience, junkier than the bowls of sugary cereal my parents would never serve.

"Anyone can experience any of those things on any day!" I pointed out. "And have you ever noticed how all the signs of the zodiac are supposedly tied to certain character traits like 'shy but social' or 'patient but impulsive'?"

Ella sulkily swirled her spoon around the bowl of pink milk. "What's your point?"

"They're totally opposite traits, giving you zero personality at all!"

Ella wouldn't listen to logic.

"I like knowing the stars are looking out for me."

"*I'm* looking out for you."

Ella said nothing, half shrugged, and swiped at her phone.

Mom says too many clients end up in her office because they prefer horoscopes, tarot, and palm readings over common sense.

So I really wasn't looking forward to number 26. That is, until Kaytee came along and got so excited about our back-to-back birthdays.

"You're a Libra," I inform her.

"What's a Libra?" she asks.

"The scales," I say.

"Scales? Who wants to be scales?"

"Scales are well-balanced," I say.

Kaytee flips herself over and starts walking around on her hands as if to prove just how well-balanced she is.

"You appreciate the finer things in life," I continue, "and you get along with all different types of people so you're supersocial. And you're always up for new experiences."

"La-di-da-da!" She hops back to her feet. "No duh! That's totally me!"

She says it in a jokey way. And despite what I know about the one-sign-fits-all vagueness of horoscopes, that description suits Kaytee perfectly. I mean, she *literally* balances her entire body on her hands. And her bedroom is the fanciest I've ever seen in real life. She obviously gets along with everyone, because she's still talking to me.

"What are you?" she asks.

"I'm a Virgo."

"What's a Virgo?" she asks.

"A pure woman," I say.

"Ooooh!" Kaytee applauds. "That's a good one to get! Way better than scales!"

"Scales aren't so bad," I say. "You could have gotten the lowly crab or the stinky goat."

Or the deadly scorpion. Morgan's November birthday suits her poisonous personality. Ella is Aquarius, the water bearer. Just perfect for posing at the pool in her teeny bikini.

"So what sort of person are you?" she asks.

Ickface! Ickface! Ickface!

"Cautious and quiet."

I have to admit that's a pretty accurate description of my personality. You know, as far as generic fake pseudoscientific analysis goes.

"So Libras like me are all about seeing and doing and *go go going*!" Kaytee twirls in a circle as she talks. "Virgos like you think everything through before doing or saying something you might regret. Opposites attract, right?"

Kaytee is literally and figuratively putting a positive spin on our differences. I'm thinking if the Libra in her likes to try new things, maybe she'll be willing to try them with me. I open my backpack and show her the book I've come to live by this summer.

"Have you ever heard of *The Book of Awesome for Awesome Girls*?" I ask.

"Nope!" she replies cheerfully.

I'm not surprised. Though the Awesome Girls Team says "awesome girls aren't born that way, they're made," I bet Kaytee's awesomeness was obvious from day one. Normally I'd never think someone as awesome-from-birth as Kaytee would be interested in my To Do List. I've got a cover story just in case though. One that is mostly true.

"My parents are strict and won't let me have my own phone so . . ."

"Mine too!" Kaytee gives me a feisty, friendly shove.

"Really?" I ask.

"Really!" she answers. "And my parents won't let me go on Fotobomb or any of the socials . . ."

"Mine either!"

This is maybe the luckiest day of my life! I don't have to worry about Kaytee calling me a baby because I don't have a phone. But does that mean she'll go for the book? I tweak the truth just in case.

"My parents told me if I make my way through the whole book before the end of the calendar year, I might be able to prove to them that I'm focused and responsible enough to have my own phone."

Okay. So maybe that's a little more than tweaking the truth. But what's the harm? Especially when Kaytee is responding so positively.

"There's one hundred To Dos," I say. "And I started at the end of June, which gives me a little over six months."

Kaytee is listening carefully, so I continue.

"That's roughly point five five five or a little over half a To Do per day to get done by my December thirty-first deadline."

"Point five five five?" Kaytee asks. "How do you do half a To Do?"

"Some take longer than others," I say. "I try to cross off one To Do every other day. That's a better way to break it down. When school starts, my pace will slow down a bit so I'm trying to get ahead now . . ."

I've clearly spent too much time strategizing. And yet Kaytee doesn't look doubtful at all. She looks . . . determined. To see and do and go go go!

"That's totally to-doable!" Kaytee exclaims. "That phone is yours!"

This is all going way better than I could have predicted when Mrs. Ray opens the front door to announce her presence on the premises.

"Hello, Sophie!"

She's dressed down today. Her hair is pulled back in a ponytail just like Kaytee's, and she wears a sporty tank and knee-length yoga pants. Dad says most of the moms dressed in yoga pants don't go to yoga. He calls them Frappuccino pants instead. I don't know about those other coffee-drinking moms, but Mrs. Ray looks fit, like she could walk on her hands too.

"I was just about to invite Sophie inside our comfortably air-conditioned home," Kaytee says. "Is that okay with you, Mother dear?"

She asks the question in a clipped British accent. I bet Mrs. Ray lectured Kaytee about inviting friends over without her permission after I left that first day. The goofy voice is Kaytee's way of breaking any leftover mother-daughter tension. It works.

"Of course it's okay, Daughter dear," Mrs. Ray replies in a British accent of her own that isn't as good as Kaytee's but still pretty good for a mom.

Mrs. Ray gently tugs on Kaytee's ponytail as she bounds past her. Kaytee reaches up for a quick tug of her mom's ponytail in return. As they joke with ease, I pull at the hair curling under my earlobe. Part of me wishes it was long enough for a ponytail, just to join in on all the tugging fun.

SAME DIFFERENCE

I HEAR THE GRUNTING ABOUT HALFWAY UP THE STAIRS TO KAYTEE'S room.

"My antisocial, not-get-alongable, likes-the-grosser-things-in-life brother."

When we reach the top I see Alex dangling from a metal bar set up in the bedroom doorway across the hall from Kaytee's. His eyes are shut tight and his entire body is tensed up in the struggle to pull himself up one more time.

Kaytee puts her finger to her lips like *Shhhhh.*

She stealthily tiptoes up to her brother . . .

. . . and attacks him with armpit tickles!

"AAAAAAAAAAH!"

Alex loses his grip on the bar and flops to the floor.

"HAHAHAHAHAHA!"

Kaytee makes a break for her room, pushing me to go

fasterfasterfaster, but her twin recovers, tackles his sister, and takes her down on the flowered rug right outside the safety of her bedroom door. Before I can even process what's happening, Alex straddles Kaytee and pins her arms over her head. He's got unlimited retaliatory armpit-tickling access!

"REVENGE IS MIIIIIIIIIIINE!"

"LEXI, NOOOOOOOO!"

"I TOLD YOU TO STOP CALLING ME THAT!"

They're both half yelling, half laughing.

I'm fully freaking out!

Alex isn't much bigger than Kaytee, but he's way stronger. Plus I bet he's got years of boy-on-boy aggression to his advantage. I'm afraid he'll hurt her, even if it isn't on purpose. And if I just let it happen, doesn't that make me as much to blame as Alex?

"GET OFF!"

"NO WAY!"

I don't know if they're just messing around or mad at each other or what. It's hard to tell with siblings sometimes and I don't have any personal experience in this area.

"SURRENDER!"

"NEVER!"

Alex puts Kaytee in a headlock. I'm convinced he's going to choke her to death and I'm about to run downstairs to get Mrs. Ray to intervene when, as suddenly as it started—it's over.

"I've trained you well," Alex says.

Sweaty, red-faced, and breathing hard, he hops off Kaytee and extends his hand to help her up. Kaytee takes his hand but spits into it first! Ewwww! There are more germs in the human mouth than anywhere else on the body. And I mean *anywhere* else. I don't know why any girl is in a rush to have any boy's mouth anywhere near her own. I know this is an unpopular opinion for an almost twelve-year-old, but kissing is gross. How will I ever *not* think about the eighty million microorganisms swapped between lips?

"And *I'm* the one in military prison for bad behavior," Alex says.

He brings his sister in for a hug, but only long enough to wipe Kaytee's spit on the back of her tank top. There's way too much back-and-forth brother/sister antagonism to keep track of!

"It's not a military prison," Kaytee corrects, shoving him off. "It's an all-boys country day school."

"Same difference."

Alex sticks a hand under his T-shirt and squeezes a rapid triplet of armpit farts.

I'm still stunned by the death-match intensity of what I've just witnessed. But this kind of thing must happen all the time because Kaytee is unfazed.

"Are you okay?" I ask.

"Oh, what? That?" Kaytee asks, thumbing in the direction of the hall. "That's classic Lexi."

"I TOLD YOU TO STOP CALLING ME THAT!" Alex shouts from the other side of the closed door.

"I TOLD YOU TO STOP EAVESDROPPING!" Kaytee shouts back.

Kaytee looks down at her tank tops, which are all stretched and hanging off her shoulders from the battle.

"Ugh," she says. "I need to change. Do you mind?" Kaytee asks. "It'll just take a second."

Ella and I used to change in front of each other all the time, but that's because we'd known each other forever. I can't blame Kaytee for wanting some privacy in front of someone she just met. She obviously isn't as comfortable around me as I already am around her.

"Sure thing," I say.

I slip out into the hallway to wait. And though the moment shouldn't feel awkward, it sort of does because Alex is hanging from his chin-up bar right across the narrow hallway.

"She's shy," Alex says.

Kaytee? Shy?

Kaytee doesn't seem the insecure type, but maybe her parents don't emphasize inner beauty as much as mine do. Her modesty definitely doesn't fit her otherwise bold personality. Too many clients end up in my mom's office because they develop distorted perceptions of their appearance in early childhood.

Alex drops to the ground, strikes a bodybuilder pose.

"I'm not."

Then he laughs his madman laugh and slams his bedroom door. A moment later, Kaytee swings open her door, grabs my arm, and pulls me back inside.

LIFE RAFT

KAYTEE HAS CHANGED INTO A *KAYTEE K. KRAZY LIFE SO FAR TOUR*
T-shirt and charges right back to our conversation like nothing even
happened.

"So what will we To Do today?" Kaytee asks, paging through
the book.

"I've already done a lot of the most challenging To Dos."

"You started with the hardest ones?" she asks.

Yes, because the hardest ones require more time. And if there's
anything I've had too much of this summer, it's time.

But that's not what I tell her.

"Of course," I say instead. "That's just smart strategy. I got
most of the tough ones out of the way first so the list wouldn't
seem so impossible."

Except for *the* impossible one.

"It's like the Kaytee K. song," Kaytee says. *"Never impossible! Always I'm possible!"*

Kaytee puts her arms out in front of her like a superhero soaring through the sky. Just like the video. I wish the inspirational lyrics worked on me.

"What were some of the toughest ones?" she asks.

"Hmm. Let's see." I thumb through the book. "Like number twenty-three. 'Change a Car Tire.'" I skip over Impossible Number 45. "Or number eighty-eight. 'Build a Life Raft.'"

"You built a life raft?!"

"Uh-huh," I say. "With a bunch of branches and some twine. I doubt it was seaworthy, but I did it and crossed it off the list."

Number 88 took almost a week to complete. The best To Do so far, by far.

"Why would you build a life raft?" she asks.

Because I had nothing else better to do, I think.

"Do you plan on getting shipwrecked anytime soon?" she asks.

On the lonely island of misfit seventh graders, I think.

"If it's in the book, it's on my list." I upend the Kathy's Krafts shopping bag, and dozens of embroidery flosses tumble to the rug. "Number seventeen!"

This is another To Do I'd avoided until now. Can you imagine anything more depressing than a friendless girl making friendship bracelets?

There's a half dozen shades of pink and Kaytee seems determined to use every single one of them. I go for Villa Academy colors: green, gray, and tan. My parents won't get the significance of this silent protest, but it pleases me to think about it anyway.

Even though it's my To Do List, Kaytee ends up guiding me through the bracelet-making process. For someone with kiddie bounce-house levels of energy, she's a surprisingly patient teacher. This is good because I'm a terrible bracelet maker, even with the simplest pattern. I'm usually great at following directions, but my manual dexterity is lacking. I can't help but think how much better it might be if my parents allowed me to take piano lessons. Not that it matters because I would've quit them by now anyway.

"So what are you into?"

It's as if Kaytee can read my mind.

"What do you mean?"

"Well, you know I loooove Kaytee K. and dancing and dolphins and overall fabooshness," she says, gesturing around the blinged-out room. "So, like, what are *you* into?"

I shrug.

"Okay, Miss Cautious and Quiet," she says, setting down her bracelet. "Lightning round of favorites! Ice cream flavor? Mine's bubble gum!"

I used to think it was butter pecan until MorganElla said only mothbally old ladies like butter pecan.

"I like bubble gum too," I say.

Kaytee high-fives me.

"Book?"

I used to think it was *The Dragonologist Chronicles* until

MorganElla said only babies read make-believe stories about dragons.

"It's hard to choose just one."

"I know, right? But if I had to pick just one book, mine's definitely Kaytee K.'s autobiography."

I'm admiring Kaytee for how easily she expresses her opinions, unafraid that I might disagree, or worse, flat out tell her that her likes and dislikes are all wrong.

"Favorite subject in school?"

I was happiest in Mrs. Mapleton's music class until . . .

"Um, I don't know . . ."

"You're just being modest. I can tell you're supersmart. I bet you're really good at science."

I *am* really good at science. But I wouldn't say it's my favorite unless Dad's asking. There's a big difference between being really good at something and being really *into* something.

"My favorite is language arts," Kaytee adds.

Kaytee is the type of girl who volunteers to read her essays out loud, while girls like me slink low in their seats and hope the teacher forgets they're there.

"Favorite hobby, like the thing you can do for hours and hours and never, ever get bored?"

I used to think it was singing.

Until . . .

I shrug again.

Kaytee accepts I'm not very good at the Lightning Round game. She changes her technique.

"I've never been to New York City, have you?" Kaytee asks.

This I can answer. My parents have brought me along on trips to New York City since I was an infant. It's a fact, not an opinion.

"Dad takes me to museums," I say. "Mom takes me to Broadway musicals."

The museums balance out the musicals, though not recently, because I haven't begged to go.

"I'm so jealous! That's the best part about moving to New Jersey," she says. "Being so close to New York City!"

I'd like to think my home state has more to offer than its nearness to a cool city in another state. We've got oceans and mountains and forests and many, many malls. But I decide to let the slight slide. At least Kaytee hasn't joked about toxic waste dumps or mocked me for a "Joisey" accent I don't even have. That's better than most newbies to the area.

"So what's the best Broadway show you've ever seen?" she asks.

And just like that, I'm back to thinking what I don't want to think about.

Wicked. The Lion King. Les Miz. Two summers ago Ella had the great idea to arrange all my Broadway Playbills in a grid on my wall. *Matilda. Phantom. Dear Evan Hansen.* I would've never thought to do that and I loved the way the black-and-yellow logo popped against my white walls. They're now stuffed in a box in my closet, covers torn in my hurry to take them down.

"Hello?" Kaytee snaps her fingers in my face. "Favorite Broadway show?"

The reminder literally puts a lump in my throat, like a huge wad of peanut butter and spelt crackers without any soy milk to wash it down.

"It's hard to say."

I think it's starting to dawn on Kaytee just how much is hard for me to say. But what if one wrong answer clues her into my true Ickface identity?

"I saw *Wicked* on the national tour when it came to DC, but it's just not the same as seeing it on Broadway, you know?"

I know. I really, really know.

In fifth grade, Mrs. Mapleton encouraged Ella and me to perform a song from *Wicked* called "For Good" for the talent show. It's about how friendship changes us. Maybe not for the better, but forever. *For good.* Back then I didn't get the double meaning. Now I do.

Ella is gone.

For good.

And her absence hurts so much I'm crushed by the weight of every single feeling in every single song I've ever sung.

I hurt like Elphaba without Glinda.

I hurt like Eponine without Marius.

I hurt like Timon without Pumbaa.

"Sophie?"

Kaytee is snapping her fingers in front of my face.

"I'm, like, the last person on earth who hasn't seen *Hamilton*!"

I hurt like Alexander Hamilton after his duel with Aaron Burr.

It takes me a moment to return to the room.

"Mom's the one who's into musicals," I answer slowly. "I get dragged along because I'm an only child. Music kind of goes in one ear and out the other with me."

Kaytee has no way of knowing that nothing is further from the truth because I couldn't bring myself to answer her question. *Favorite hobby, like the thing you can do for hours and hours and never, ever get bored?*

"How about you?" I ask. "Do you play the piano downstairs?"

Kaytee twiddles her fingers in a brief but virtuosic air piano performance.

"I started taking lessons a few years ago because my parents wanted me to learn how to sit still and concentrate. I've got excellent hand-eye coordination but, like, zero true musical talent. Like, I can't sing at all. I sound like a constipated hippopotamus."

And then Kaytee breaks into an awful version of an old Kaytee K. song.

"*I am, I am, I am . . . Amazing, blazing, krazing . . .*"

I'm supposed to laugh, so I do. But I'm too disappointed to find genuine humor in her horribly off-key performance. For a moment there, I thought I might get revenge with a new duet partner.

Kaytee enthusiastically changes the subject.

"Let's put on our bracelets!"

Kaytee could sell hers at a boutique in downtown Stockton Square. Despite my best efforts on the most basic striped design, mine is all wonky and wrong-looking. Without hesitating, she takes my hand and wraps her perfect pink-on-pink-on-six-different-pinks arrowhead pattern bracelet around my wrist. If I had known we were making them for each other, I would have tried even harder! Kaytee deserves better than my asymmetrical green, gray, and tan mess.

Kaytee misinterprets my hesitation.

"Oh! You made yours for another friend!"

Another friend. Ha!

"No," I insist. "Villa Academy colors. For your first day of school tomorrow."

"Ohhh." Kaytee obviously has no idea what Villa Academy's colors are. "Perfect! Thank you!"

For her sake, I tie it loosely so it will fall off fast. That way she won't have to explain her ugly accessory in front of her fancy Villa Academy classmates.

I got it from my Ickface neighbor! She's totally obsessed with me! I'm afraid to take it off because she'll start stalking me or something . . .

"Maybe *I* can prove to my parents that I'm focused and responsible. Maybe *I* can convince my parents to buy *me* a phone . . ."

Kaytee's voice lifts and trails off like she's dropping a hint, but I'm not picking it up. She waits a beat before getting more direct.

"So, if it's cool with you, I'd love to work on the rest of these To Dos together," Kaytee says. "On weekends. Or after school. You know, when you're not busy hanging out with all your other friends."

All my other friends.

I need to redirect her attention. If we're going to discuss friends, let's talk about hers. I pick up a framed photo on her nightstand. It looks like it was taken a few years ago at a Halloween or costume party. Kaytee is in a white rhinestoned jumpsuit and sunglasses.

"Elvis?" I ask.

"Everyone thought that!" She looks genuinely offended. "I'm Kaytee K. in the 'Las Vegas Loca Vida' video!"

I feel like such a dork for not knowing that.

On one side of her is an Asian girl with a Hogwarts scarf wrapped around her neck. On the other side is a Black girl wearing a Dragonologist headlamp.

"Are these your friends from Virginia?" I ask.

Kaytee blinks rapidly, like I've flashed the center stage spotlight. It takes a moment for her to adjust.

"Yep! That's Allie and Gracie!"

She says it in a squeakier tone than normal.

"You must miss them," I say.

She nods once slowly.

"I do."

She takes the picture frame out of my hand and sets it back down on the table.

"So," she says, "I'd like to meet them."

"Who?"

"All *your* other friends!"

All my other friends.

"What are all your other friends doing today?" she asks. "I mean, why are you hanging out with me instead of them?"

I need to explain why I'm not hanging out with *all my other friends.*

Kaytee is determined to know about *all my other friends.*

Kaytee isn't going to Mercer Middle.

Kaytee will never meet *all my other friends*.

All my other friends can be whatever I want them to be.

"My best friends are Morgan and Ella," I begin. "Maybe you've heard of them?"

Kaytee shakes her head.

"Well, they're amazing singers. Ella plays ukulele too. Anyway, they're superpopular on YouTube and all the socials and are going to be totally famous one day."

It's miraculous, really, how easily the words come out. Once my blabbermouth starts, it won't stop.

"And my other best friend, Maddy? She's a marketing genius and is totally setting them up for global multiplatform domination."

"Whoa," Kaytee says when I'm finished. "Your friends sound so cool. I'm lucky you had time to spend with me today!"

For once, I'm the lucky one here. Lucky that Kaytee will never know the truth about *all my other friends*. *All my other friends* can be whatever I want them to be. Making me the kind of girl I can only be in my imagination. The kind of girl who is faboosh in Kaytee's eyes. I've somehow managed to pull off this charade for a few days. Is it possible to fool her . . . forever?

"Thanks for making me feel at home here," she says.

"You're welcome," I say.

Thank you, I think.

Kaytee helped me build a second life raft today. This one is made out of a silly book and embroidery floss and will hopefully help me survive the loneliest year of my life.

PART
TWO

FIRST DAY

ELLA IS AFRAID OF THE DARK. OR MAYBE SHE ISN'T ANYMORE. BUT she used to be when we were still best friends. We slept over at each other's houses anywhere from one to four times a month between kindergarten and the summer before sixth grade, so this is something I know for a fact about Ella, from many, many opportunities to observe for myself. But just because it was true then doesn't mean it's still true now. Maybe in the past year she outgrew her fear of the dark, just like she phased out of Girl Scouts and underwater karaoke.

And me.

Ella had a very simple and specific strategy for dealing with the dark. She'd pull the covers over her head and burrow herself deep under the duvet so there were no signs of an innocently sleeping girl from the outside.

"If I can't see It," she'd reason from inside her goose-down fortress, "It can't see me."

"It" was a shadowy, sinister monster that snuck up on unsuspecting sleeping girls and . . . well . . . Ella wasn't sure what would happen next.

"But I'm not going to find out!"

I knew Ella had nothing to be afraid of because monsters don't exist. Mom said Ella's fears stem from the lack of a father figure in her life. Ella's dad left her mom when she was a toddler. The only memories she has of him aren't even her own, just passed-down stories from her older sister, Lauren. I never wanted Ella to feel bad about not having a dad around. I wanted to be a good friend, so I pretended to be scared of It too.

"There's safety in numbers," I'd say, scrunching next to my best friend beneath the blankets. I've listened and watched and, yes, even felt the rise and fall of Ella's breath as she fell asleep beside me hundreds of times. I never let myself drift off until I knew she was slumbering soundly. Together, under the covers, Ella and I were safe from the invisible, imaginary menace of It.

If I can't see It, It can't see me.

Only now, as I march through the front entrance of Mercer Middle School on my first day of seventh grade—pushing through the crowded crush, head down, 100 percent focused on my mission to get to homeroom unnoticed—do I realize I've applied the same nonsense logic to my own deepest fears.

If I can't see It, It can't see me.

My It isn't anonymous. My It has a name:

MorganElla.

I am so glad Kaytee isn't here to see me so shook by a monster who applies her mascara one microscopic eyelash at a time.

I prepared myself for seventh grade by:

- Memorizing the school's floor plan so I don't get lost in the halls
- Asking Dad to order all the required school supplies (including folders, binders, pencils, pens, highlighters, etc.) as described in the welcome letter
- Creating a color-coordinated system of folders and binders organized by subject
- *Quietly* asking Mom to buy two more bras, which led to a mortifying dinnertime bullet-point discussion about the hypothalamus, hormones, and body odor until Dad begged her to stop talking

But none of this has prepared me for the dreaded inevitable. I avoided It all summer but It didn't go away. All this time, MorganElla has been alive and well and waiting for an opportunity to attack. I'm almost at the staircase when I'm struck down.

"Fotobombed! Ugly Outfit of the Day!"

I spin around and see MorganElla and Maddy, all with their phones up and aimed at me. They're dressed almost identically in dark skinny jeans and neon sleeveless tees.

PEACE, says Ella's shirt.

LOVE, says Morgan's shirt.

HAPPY, says Maddy's shirt.

It still stuns me to see Ella at the heart of this peppy firing squad. Even after all the pain she's caused me, my first instinct is to ask, *"How are you?"*

"Ummm . . . Sophie? Whole Foods wants its moldy cheese back." Morgan sniffs.

"Ick. Stinks like Roquefort too."

Thanks to Mom's puberty bullet points, I know that isn't true. If anything, I smell like tree tea oil deodorant. But I don't say that. I don't say anything. I'm trying too hard not to panic.

Inhale.

Expand the belly.

Count to three.

Exhale.

Squeeze the belly.

Count to three.

"Ugh. What's a Roquefort?" jokes Ella in a ditzy voice.

"Duh! A moldy cheese that looks exactly like Sophie's shirt."

I want to point out Eco/Echo's trademark marbleized design, as seen in last month's *Teen Vogue*. I want to tell Ella how this shirt is making the world a better place. But I can't get it out, so all they can see is an off-white cotton shirt shot through with streaks of a color that, well, if Kaytee's walls are more green than blue, then this is more blue than green.

Just like moldy cheese.

I'll never look at this shirt the same way again.

"Ugh," Ella says in an even ditzier voice. "How do you even *spell* 'Roquefort'?"

I still have to fight the impulse to help her.

Does Ella remember the many hours I sat at her kitchen table drilling our word lists to help her prepare for our weekly quizzes? Does she remember the countless embarrassed tears she cried when she couldn't spell more than half the words correctly? Does she remember how I comforted her by listing all the different ways to be smart?

No.

No.

No.

MorganElla and Maddy make their way down the ground-floor hallway, tapping at screens, laughing at me. And the only thing that keeps me from running right out the front door and pleading my case for homeschooling to my parents is this:

MorganElla is not walking in the direction of the stairs.

The monster isn't headed for the second floor.

MorganElla is in the Cool House.

I am in the Uncool House.

This is where It should be. This is where I should be.

"Hey, Sophie!"

It's Harumi and Sofie-with-an-F from Shadybrook Elementary.

"Are you House Two too?"

They are also where they should be. Harumi and Sofie-with-an-F are nice girls. I'm sure they make totally fine friends for each other. But since I've become friends with Kaytee, these two seem . . . well . . . duller than ever. I'm not saying it to be mean. I'm saying it because it's true.

Like MorganElla and Maddy, they coordinated their back-to-school outfits. Unlike the other girls, Harumi and Sofie-with-an-F are wearing floral dresses, long cardigans, and sneakers. Cool and Uncool House styles vary, but with my moldy cheese shirt I don't fit in either way.

"Lemme see!"

Harumi snatches my schedule out of my hand. A quick scan confirms that either she or Sofie-with-an-F or both are in all my classes. I'd spent so much energy worrying about *not* being with MorganElla that I hadn't given much thought at all about who I *would* be with.

"We haven't seen you since school got out," Sofie-with-an-F says. "How was your summer?"

"Where did you go? What did you do? Who did you hang out with?"

Harumi is more direct than Sofie-with-an-F.

It hadn't occurred to me that anyone would care enough to ask how I spent my summer.

It hadn't occurred to me that I would have an acceptable answer.

"A new girl named Kaytee moved next door," I say. "We totally bonded and she's, like, my best friend now, but it's so annoying because she's going to Villa Academy."

I don't mention that we only spent the last week of summer vacation together.

I don't mention that I spent the previous eleven weeks working on a To Do List.

Alone.

Alone.

Alone.

"Sweet," Sofie-with-an-F says.

"So what's she like?" presses Harumi.

"Well, she's from Virginia . . ."

I'm so relieved to be able to tell them all about Kaytee as we join the noisy crowd of nameless students heading for the stairwell.

"And she's a huge Kaytee K. fan and a dancer and superstylish and . . ."

Just thinking about my new friend makes me feel less alone.

Alone.

Alone.

"She sounds cool," Harumi says.

"Yeah," Sofie-with-an-F agrees.

"She is," I say.

My pain gives way to brief, bittersweet relief.

It doesn't last for long though. I have a sinking feeling my first brutal encounter with MorganElla marks the beginning of what will be a very long, very Icky year.

DIFFERENT VERSIONS

KAYTEE AND I AGREED TO GET TOGETHER AFTER SCHOOL TO DISCUSS
our first days. Villa Academy is a bit of a drive, so she'll leave
earlier and return later than I will every day. There's at least an
hour before I can see her, so I head to my house instead of hers.
I approach the lock as quietly as I always do, so my entrance won't
disturb Dad. The door swings open before I turn the key.

"Welcome home!"

My parents have never greeted me at the door after school. I
can't remember the last time my mom was even home after school.
Or the last time Dad emerged from his office before dinner. This
is a very special occasion. They are very eager to hear about my
first day of middle school.

"What are your teachers like?" asks Mom.

"What will you learn this year?" asks Dad.

Fortunately, their questions are easy to answer. I won't be a disappointment. We head to the kitchen, and over a snack of avocado toast, I tell them what they want to hear.

I tell them my science teacher's experience with teaching the basic properties of physics to seventh grade honors students gives Dr. Dawson an edge whenever he enters Albert Einstein look-alike contests.

I tell them my social studies teacher, Mr. Schwartzman, is barely older than my dad's university students but makes up in enthusiasm what he lacks in experience. He spent his summer backpacking throughout India, Thailand, and Indonesia, which gives him a whole new awesome perspective on the impact of Hinduism, Buddhism, and Islam on Southeast Asian politics and culture.

I tell them my language arts teacher, Ms. Salinger, isn't related to the famous author of the classic novel we will read later in the year. She's always felt a deep connection with his work and rereads the novel along with every class even though it's been on the curriculum for two decades. Each new crop of students makes the material feel fresh.

I tell them my pre-algebra teacher, Ms. Hernandez, got her degree from Dad's university and quit her job on Wall Street to encourage middle schoolers to love math. Her room is decorated with jokey posters like:

3 OUT OF 2 PEOPLE HAVE TROUBLE WITH FRACTIONS

I tell them my Spanish teacher, Señora Martin, speaks five languages: English, Spanish, French, German, and Dragonese. The last one was a joke, but there's actually a whole *Dragonologist*

Chronicles Handbook devoted to studying it. I don't mention that I had briefly considered buying it in paperback until I remembered I'd have no one to speak Dragonese with so I settled on *The Book of Awesome for Awesome Girls* instead. She wants us to pronounce her name as it would be by Spanish-language speakers: Mar-TEEN. In French it would be: Mar-TAN. German: MAH-tin. Dragonese: Mar-SNICKITY-tin-SNACK.

"What an inspiring group of educators!" Mom says.

"Our tax dollars at work," Dad says.

They are pleased. Especially Dad, who goes back to his office and shuts the door. Mom stays behind.

"What about the other girls from Shadybrook Elementary?"

Oh no. Mom wants me to answer tougher questions about friends I don't have whose names she can't remember or never knew at all. It's only a matter of time before she asks about the only one worth asking about.

"How's Ella doing these days?" Her brow crumples with concern. "Still hanging out with a bad crowd?"

That's what I told Mom last year when she finally looked up from her caseloads long enough to ask why Ella wasn't calling, carpooling, or coming over for sleepovers anymore. *Ella is hanging out with a bad crowd.* I knew Mom would accept this oversimplified version of the truth. Too many clients end up in her office because of bad crowds.

I do not tell Mom about the most unexpected part of my day, when Ella arrived late as usual and alone—as *never*—to my last-period gym class. I can't remember the last time I saw her unattached to Morgan. She seemed a little lost, to be honest. But any sympathy I might have had for her vanished when I remembered her comparing me to stinky cheese just a few hours before. I am hopelessly uncoordinated so phys ed is already my least favorite part of the day. It's definitely the biggest threat to my GPA. And now I have to waste even more energy trying to avoid my ex–best friend taunting me in the locker room for wearing a toddler undershirt I don't even wear anymore . . . ? Maybe I can get some kind of medical exemption . . . ?

"Sophie!"

From her tone, I can tell Mom has been talking at me, but I haven't heard a single thing she's said.

"I asked if there's anyone you want to invite along to the beach house this year? Your birthday is only a few weeks away," Mom is saying. "The big twelve. Last stop before teendom . . ."

Like I need reminding. I change the subject.

"What are you doing home anyway?" I ask, crushing a lumpy bit of avocado with the last crust of bread.

I expect her to tell me something like how the pregnant pot smoker skipped her court-mandated check-in and is now on the run from the law. I am wrong.

"I'm switching up my schedule so I can be home more often in the afternoons."

I push my plate away.

"Why?" I ask. "Dad's here. I don't need babysitting." Then, channeling Kaytee I add, "Girls my age don't need babysitters. They *are* babysitters."

"Of course," Mom says, taking off her glasses. "But too many clients end up in my office because—"

I don't want to hear it right now. Thankfully, I'm saved by the doorbell.

"That's Kaytee!" I jump off my kitchen stool. "Gotta go!"

I rush to meet her at the front door. She's already changed out of her uniform and into shorts and a Kaytee K. LAS VEGAS LOCA VIDA tee.

"Hey!"

Kaytee takes a step back to admire my first-day-of-school outfit. I hope I haven't let her down. After a beat, she grabs my hands and shakes them silly like maracas.

"I love your shirt!"

Without question, this is the highlight of my day. But I can't tell her that.

Like my parents, Kaytee will get a highly edited take on Mercer Middle School, one especially tailored for the audience. Unlike my parents' version though, what Kaytee will hear contains very little truth.

"Seriously," Kaytee gushes, "it brings out the blue in your eyes!"

"Ella and Morgan said the same exact thing!"

What Kaytee doesn't know will only help our friendship grow.

WHAT I LIKE ABOUT MIDDLE SCHOOL

I LIKE RULES. I LIKE OBJECTIVES AND GUIDELINES AND EXPECTATIONS. I like seating charts, especially those arranged alphabetically. I like knowing Harumi or Sofie-with-an-F or both will sit next to me in all the classes without assigned seats.

I like the predictability of teachers, whose quirks are often off-putting at first until I get used to them.

I like knowing Dr. Dawson will run his hands through his hair as he talks about forces and motion, so I'm no longer distracted as the white cloud on top of his head gets wilder and wilder throughout the period until it resembles an atomic bomb blast when the bell rings.

I like knowing Ms. Salinger's bracelets will clang against the blackboard when she writes vocabulary words and their Latin and Greek roots, so I don't jump and bang my knees against the underside of the desk anymore when it happens.

I like knowing Ms. Hernandez will accurately predict the daily lunch menu based on the greasy aromas piped into her classroom via an unfortunately placed cafeteria ventilation duct.

I like making connections between my To Dos and the seventh grade curriculum. Like number 6 ("Make a Paper Cup Speaker") clearly demonstrates Dr. Dawson's lecture on how electricity and magnets are related. Or number 39 ("Design a Map of an Imaginary Planet") illustrates Mr. Schwartzman's lessons about the influence of topography and geography on culture. Even number 81 ("Watch a Movie in a Foreign Language with Subtitles") got me used to hearing a lot of strange-sounding words in Señora Mar-TEEN's class.

But I never raise my hand to share these observations.

That was the old me.

The girl who had a voice.

WHAT I DON'T LIKE ABOUT MIDDLE SCHOOL

I HATE THE CHAOTIC IN-BETWEENS.

I hate the lawless hallways.

I was wrong about students from House One and House Two never crossing paths outside except for gym. Dramatic reunions happen in the hallways before and after every class period, as friends cruelly separated by the random placement in different Houses pass one another while entering/exiting the school's so-called shared spaces: the specials (tech, art, health, etc.), the gym, the cafeteria. Besties who haven't seen each other since OMIGOD!!! FOREVER!!!! have just a few seconds to exchange a lifetime's worth of gossip:

"He texted me so I texted back . . ."

"Our selfie got fifty likes so we totally have to . . ."

"But how long do I wait until I text again . . . ?"

"I can't believe she unfollowed me . . ."

Ella is as committed to ignoring me in gym class as I am to ignoring her. But MorganElla seizes any opportunity to humiliate me, no matter how brief.

"Fotobomb!"

"Ugliest Outfit of the Day!"

"Ickface breaks the Internet!"

These short seconds loom larger and last longer than all the hours before and after. It doesn't matter how well the rest of my day has gone, how many conversations I've had with Harumi and Sofie-with-an-F, how many connections I've made between my To Do List and my lessons. As soon as I step into House One and Two's shared spaces, I'm a target.

"Fotobomb!"

"Hashtag Ickface!"

"It's like she doesn't even know how sad she is."

MorganElla means "sad" as in "to be pitied," not sad as in "unhappy." But she's wrong. I know exactly how sad I am at school in both senses of the word. And I know it because of how different I feel when I'm working on my To Dos with Kaytee.

THE COOL HOUSE

WE'RE IN KAYTEE'S GARAGE. SUPPOSEDLY FINISHING UP OUR TIE-DYED T-shirts (number 55) we'd left to set overnight. We're not making much progress because Kaytee is way more interested in discussing what I'm most desperate not to talk about.

"It's too bad Ella, Morgan, and Maddy can't come over today," Kaytee says, hanging up her damp shirt to dry. "You sure you don't want to ask again?"

I had prepared for this possibility, so I answer as coolly as I can.

"They're all superbusy after school, you know, filming and posting videos and, um, curating their social media profiles."

This is all true. But it has nothing to do with why we aren't tie-dying T-shirts together. Kaytee will never know that part of it. No harm done.

"I guess global multiplatform domination doesn't come easy," Kaytee says.

"I guess it doesn't."

"I still can't believe your parents wouldn't switch you into the Cool House with all your friends," Kaytee says. "That's so harsh."

"I know, right?"

Kaytee is very interested in how the House system works. Everyone at Mercer Middle School knows House One is the Cool House. When someone asks what House you're in and you answer, "House One," the response is, "Oooh, lucky! That's the Cool House." If you answer, "House Two," the response is, "Oh, too bad. Maybe you can switch?" It's somehow common knowledge that Ella was originally placed in House Two, but she convinced her parents to transfer her into House One so she could be with her "peer group."

"Want to hear my theory?" I ask.

Kaytee bounces up and down on her heels.

"Of course I want to hear your theory!"

Kaytee is the first person to show any interest in hearing my theory. Then again, I haven't tried it out for anyone else. I welcome the change in subject because anything is better than talking about MorganElla.

"I think the New Jersey Department of Education is conducting an experiment," I say. "And we, the students of Mercer Middle School, are the subjects."

If they aren't collecting data, they should. I think it would be very useful to know the effect our "random" placement in House One or House Two has on our futures. I'm wondering if the superiority of House One provides its students with a certain self-assuredness that will give them an edge over House Two–ers for the rest of our lives. As MorganElla says, "Confidence is way intimidating." Thirty years from now, will the evidence show that my job, my health, my relationships were all influenced by my placement in the Uncool House?

The funny thing is, not all kids in House One are cool. For example, Olivia is in House One. Olivia is definitely considered uncool because she's best friends with Harumi. A few Cool Kids were misplaced in House Two, but they are seen as the obvious exceptions and are therefore assigned, like, SUPERCOOL status because of their ability to overcome the horrible social handicap of being placed in the wrong, uncool house by the worst parents ever who won't make the switch.

"That's totally your situation, right?" Kaytee says, removing her colorful shirt from the plastic bag.

"Totally," I say. "I know other girls also stuck in House Two, so it's not like I'm all alone."

I partner up with Harumi and Sofie-with-an-F in class and sit with them at lunch but we are not a squad. We are three outcasts. The Uncool House is right where we all belong, but I can't let Kaytee know that. Whenever I get a twinge of guilt over misleading her, I think about how much worse it felt when I didn't have her as a friend at all. I can't risk losing her with the truth.

"It's not all bad news for us in House Two though," I say. "We take the stairs several times a day, and that additional exercise contributes to our cardiovascular health. And while too much sun in the summer is bad, we'll get more sunlight in the winter and studies have shown that low vitamin D levels can impair brain function. So House Two definitely has a vitamin D advantage."

Kaytee laughs but not in a mean way. She gives my shoulder an affectionate squeeze.

"Only you would consider vitamin D an upside to uncoolness!"

Coming from just about anyone else, it would sound like an insult. But Kaytee says it like she's impressed with how well I'm taking the tragic split from my clique.

"Ugh! Villa Academy is so boring compared with your school!" She shakes out her shirt. "Did you know it's pre-K to eighth grade? One big boring elementary school snoozefestarama."

I knew this already. She could've asked me.

"And it's so small there aren't enough players for a soccer team!"

I never researched private-school sports programs, so this is news to me. But I'm even more surprised to hear that soccer even matters to Kaytee. That's Alex's thing, not hers. But she's on a roll so I don't question her.

"And I never thought I'd say this, but I miss having boys around," she says. "I wish I went to a real junior high like you. Changing classes! Lockers! School dances! It's all so exciting! Don't you just love it?"

I'm squeezing every last bit of red water out of my T-shirt into the utility sink.

"Sure."

"You don't sound excited."

"Middle school is awesome!" I force a smile. "I love it!"

I wring the tee so tight, my knuckles turn white.

"It's so sweet you made shirts for Morgan, Ella, and Maddy too," she says.

I'm going home with three extra tie-dyed T-shirts to give away to a squad I don't belong to. A group selfie of me, Harumi, and Sofie-with-an-F in matching tie-dyed T-shirts would break a Fotobomb record for LOLZ and EWWZ.

Kaytee heaves a dramatic sigh.

"My shirt violates the Villa Academy dress code."

It's true. Kaytee's tie-dyed tee is the most outrageously rainbowed of all.

"You know what? Maybe I'll wear it anyway! And those Villa Academy snots can kick me right out!"

"I don't want you to get in trouble!" I protest.

"Believe me, wearing an off-limits shirt is *nothing*," Kaytee says. "My parents would probably be relieved."

Compared with Alex's issues, I guess that's true. But Kaytee doesn't elaborate. She turns off the sink. The water has been running this whole time. Too long.

"Oh no!" she exclaims. "The color washed out of your shirt and stained your skin!"

I look down at my dripping palms and almost have to laugh.

She doesn't know it, but Kaytee has literally caught this liar red-handed.

CONNECTEDNESS

I DON'T KNOW IF I'LL EVER GET USED TO MY MOM BEING HOME ON Tuesday and Thursday afternoons.

"Come in the kitchen and tell me about your day," she says before I've totally stepped inside the front door. "I made muffins."

The familiar scent of cinnamon and apples fills the air.

"Who died?"

"No one!" Mom laughs. "I made them for us!"

I take my place at the counter, where my mom has already set a muffin on a plate next to a glass of soy milk. We aren't acquaintances, but this already feels superawkward.

"So, Sophie," Mom says, "have you given any thought to joining any school clubs?"

"Not really," I say. "Kaytee and I are pretty busy with our To Do List."

We only see each other after school and on weekends, but Kaytee and I have still managed to cross off five more To Dos. She's like the most superenthusiastic Troop Leader ever. She makes even the most boring To Do (number 90: "Make a Lemon-Powered Clock") sound like the adventure of a lifetime and I'm not even getting a sash on my badge to show for it. Dad likes when we're out of the house building a compost bin (number 50, for the Rays' backyard because we already had one), as it means I'm not disturbing his writing with my "melodramatic tweenage sadness," which he says is even more bothersome than my singing used to be. He somehow got it twisted that Kaytee gave me the idea for making the compost bin, and I just let him think it's true because I don't want him to keep hating the Rays for building a house that casts a shadow over his office window.

"Don't get me wrong, Sophie, I think it's great you and Kaytee are friends. But it's important for you to be engaged at school too."

"I am engaged at school," I reply. "I'm getting straight As so far."

Even in gym.

"And I'm so happy to hear that, but I'm talking more about your"—she pauses here—"*emotional* engagement."

I silently chew my muffin. I don't think she even bothered to add the sliced apple.

"Numerous studies have shown that students who participate in extracurricular activities excel academically and have an overall feeling of connectedness to their school community."

I stuff the rest of the muffin in my mouth, just so I won't be expected to respond. It's like snacking on a cinnamon-dusted sandcastle.

Mom should be grateful I'm not moping alone in my bedroom. Kaytee is a talker and I'm a listener so whether you buy into the zodiac or not, our personalities complement each other. Just being around Kaytee quiets brainchatter and calms tummyrumble and slows heartpang to the point that I'm not just pretending to be happier for my parents' sake, I'm happier than I've been in months. The after-school and weekend happiness even carries over to my days at Mercer Middle, making them slightly less miserable than they would be otherwise. In fact, I almost felt bold enough to suggest to Dr. Dawson that we make lemon-powered clocks in class to show how a simple voltaic battery changes chemical energy into electrical energy.

Almost.

Mom thinks my friendship with Kaytee prevents me from making meaningful friendships at school. She's wrong. My friendship with Kaytee protects me from being alone.

Alone.

Alone.

"Will you at least consider a club?" Mom asks. "What are all your other friends doing after school every day?"

All my other friends.

Through the open window, I can hear Kaytee's car doors shutting in their driveway.

"Sure, Mom, I'll look into it," I reply. "But until then, can I just go over to Kaytee's?"

She nods. I hop up and am halfway to the door when she calls out to me.

"Sophie?"

I'm expecting her to say something about how too many clients end up in her office because they go adrift during adolescence. But she doesn't.

"Have fun," she says instead.

NIGHTMARE CATCHERS

EVERYTHING ABOUT MY FRIENDSHIP WITH KAYTEE IS FUN AND EASY, just as long as we avoid the subject of *all my other friends*. Usually she's way less interested than Mom in *all my other friends*. Unfortunately, today isn't one of those days.

"Are you ready for number fifty-six?" I ask.

"Making Dream Catchers" is number 56. I know there's no way a decorative configuration of twine and string can stop my middle school nightmares. But it can't *hurt* to build a trap for bad dreams, right? Just as long as I keep the dream catcher hidden from my parents so I don't have to endure a lecture about superstition versus science.

"So, Sophie," Kaytee begins. "We've been hanging out a lot since I moved here. Why haven't I met all your other friends?"

I'd hoped Kaytee would be too distracted by the To Do List that she wouldn't return to the subject of *all my other friends*. She never talks about *her* friends Allie and Gracie but I can understand why. She misses them. I bet it hurts too much to think about them. And who can blame her when I'm what New Jersey has offered in exchange?

There's no way I can tell her or Mom or Dad or anyone else the latest about me and *all my other friends*.

"Welllllll?" Kaytee is furiously tapping her foot. "Why don't you want me to meet Morgan and Ella and Maddy?"

She's all tensed up, reminding me a lot of Alex when he's flexing his muscles to show us how tough he is. For the first time since we've met, I see the twinness. I have to tell her something before she gets even madder at me . . .

I rest my head on a fluffy floor pouf.

Inhale.

I look up at the chandelier.

Expand the belly.

I count teardrop crystals.

One . . . two . . . three . . .

I don't stop at three.

I keep counting.

Four . . . five . . . six . . .

Holding . . . holding . . .

Holding it in . . .

Seven . . . eight . . . nine . . .

Teardrop crystals crying overhead . . .

TEN.

I let it all out.

"I don't bring my friends around because I don't want you to feel even worse about going to Villa Academy!"

This is pretty much 100 percent *opposite* of the truth. I don't want to make *myself* feel even worse about *not* going to Villa Academy.

"Villa Academy is known for being all about work, work, work." Which, by the way, is exactly why I wanted to go there. "And you are all about fun, fun, fun."

I sit up on the rug. Kaytee eyes me carefully.

"Villa Academy girls have a reputation for being super stuck up," I continue. "And you're nothing like that."

Kaytee must accept my excuse because she visibly relaxes.

"You're right," she says. "They *are* totally stuck up. And I'm not."

She puckers her lips, closes her eyes, and does a silly little *la-di-da-da* hip wiggle that makes me giggle. But as quickly as the mood lifts, it drops again.

"I hate school," she says.

Me too, I think.

"It's not like I thought it would be," she says.

Oh, it's exactly like I thought it would be, I think.

"I wish we were at Mercer together."

"Me too," I lie. "But it's cool that we get to hang out after school and on weekends."

Kaytee seems less enthused by this arrangement.

"Yeah," she snorts. "After school and weekends. Whatever."

Kaytee's voice has a jagged edge to it I've never heard before.

From her, anyway. But there's an uncomfortable familiarity to it. Something distinctly . . . MorganElla-like.

And just like that, the moment passes.

"I'm soooo sorry." She sighs dramatically. "I promise I'm not usually like this. I'm all over the place."

"It's okay," I say. "I bet your hormones are to blame. I always get supercranky before my period."

Kaytee doesn't know I haven't gotten my first period yet, but it seems to be the thing girls in my class say whenever they get snippy. I swear MorganElla must get her period thirty-two times a month. Another tiny lie, but I'm telling it to make her feel better. No harm done.

"SNEAK ATTACK!!!"

Alex bursts into the room like a crash of cymbals.

"GET OUT!"

"NO WAY!"

I've witnessed about a half dozen of these brother/sister skirmishes and I'm still alarmed by how quickly they start . . .

"SURRENDER!"

"NEVER!"

. . . and stop.

"Keep your wits about you," Alex says to Kaytee as he exits.

He is in and out so quickly I doubt he even noticed I was there. Kaytee casually readjusts and reties her tank tops because the knots had loosened up in the battle.

"Talk about raging hormones," says Kaytee. "He reeks like a wildebeest."

"I think he might have some aggressive tendencies," I say.

She squeezes the trigger on sugar cookie–scented room spray.

"Alex isn't aggressive," Kaytee replies. "He has impulse control issues."

That's therapist talk if I've ever heard it. And I've heard it *a lot*.

"Is that why he's going to Wilson?" I ask. "Impulse control issues?"

Kaytee sets down the spray bottle, looks away.

"He's going to Wilson," she says, her gaze drifting toward the dolphins on the wall, "because he's misunderstood."

I want to know more, but Kaytee is already setting out the materials to make our dream catchers. As she puts the feathers, beads, and suede lacing into organized piles, I wonder what will happen when Kaytee and I cross off the final To Do in *The Book of Awesome for Awesome Girls*. At the rate we're going, we'll get it done way before January first. Well, all but Impossible Number 45. And then what will we do? Is our friendship entirely built on that book? And what does it matter anyway, if I'm just a placeholder until she settles in at Villa Academy?

"What size ring do you want for your dream catcher?" Kaytee asks, fanning out small, medium, and large options.

I take the biggest one. I need all the help I can get.

KIERA WHO?

I HAVE AN OPEN INVITATION TO KAYTEE'S HOUSE. SHE COULD COME to my house but that's not what we do. Kaytee doesn't seem to mind this arrangement and neither do I. What if Dad makes a snarky remark about her house and Kaytee tells her parents and it gets all awkward and the Rays don't like me anymore?

Over the past few weeks I've become such a regular at the Rays' house that I've gotten into the habit of just showing up after school and on weekends. This welcoming attitude took some getting used to because spontaneous visits make my parents uncomfortable. They never leave a door unlocked. And they will ignore the doorbell if they aren't expecting anyone.

Usually Kaytee greets me on the front porch. When she doesn't, it's because Alex has her in a headlock on the stairs and won't let go. This Saturday morning is different though. I get all the way inside their front hall without being greeted by Kaytee or anyone else.

"Hello? Is anyone home?"

The Rays are finished moving in. No more unopened boxes line the walls. One day a professional wall hanger arrived to position all the artwork and photographs just so. I never knew there was such a thing as a professional wall hanger until Kaytee explained it to me. I made the mistake of mentioning this to Dad and he said wealthy people are the best at finding dumb ways to spend their money.

The biggest wall in the family room is devoted to pictures of Alex and Kaytee. Apparently they never went through an awkward phase when they were all ears and no teeth that no one wanted to capture on camera. I'm trying to imagine what an awkward phase for Kaytee might look like when I hear Mr. Ray and Alex talking downstairs in the basement gym. It has a bunch of weight-lifting machines and a treadmill and a stationary bike and something called a Pilates reformer that's only used by Mrs. Ray and resembles a medieval torture device. Alex spends most of his time in the basement whenever I come over. Kaytee and I will be in the kitchen making a lava lamp (number 82) and we'll jump at the *THUDDD!* of a medicine ball slammed against the wall or the *CLANGGGG!* of weights hitting the stack. We can't ever see Alex, of course, but we feel and hear and sometimes even smell his presence from wherever we are in the house. It's like he never wants us to forget he's around.

Mr. Ray and Alex like to work out together. Whenever I see Mr. Ray—which isn't often—he's either in a suit or gym clothes. Never anything in between. It's difficult to tell if Mr. Ray looks as much like Alex as Mrs. Ray looks like Kaytee because he's bald and obviously way older than his son. Mrs. Ray gives off a way more youthful vibe. Mr. Ray is tall and broad shouldered and carries himself like the kind of guy who was once athletic, but he has a bit of a belly now. I've heard him complain about not having enough time to exercise. Mr. Ray works long hours at something called a hedge fund.

I made the mistake of mentioning this to Dad because I didn't know what a hedge fund was and had the wrong idea that it involved the conservation of bushes and other greenery. Hedge fund dads are the worst of all the finance dads, and then he made me watch a documentary about the collapse of our global economy. The hedge fund bosses picked out and bought the Conspicuous Consumption Mansion for Kaytee's family so it's not their fault their house blocks my dad's afternoon light, but I'm afraid to mention that because he'll make me watch another boring documentary.

Mr. Ray and Alex are in the middle of a pretty heated conversation. Their voices are raised well above what's considered unacceptable levels in my household.

"You think I *enjoyed* getting dragged into all that drama?" Alex asks as he comes upstairs from the gym. "Like I *enjoyed* getting into that fight?"

"Violence is never the answer," Mr. Ray says.

"So I'm not allowed to defend myself?"

"You punched that boy in the face," Mr. Ray says. "Was that an appropriate response?"

Alex punched someone in the face? Forget impulse control

issues. That sounds pretty aggressive to me! No wonder Kaytee isn't worried about getting in trouble for a tie-dyed T-shirt.

"He punched first! And I shut him up, didn't I?"

"I fail to find the humor in this, Alexander."

Who did Alex punch in the face? Who punched Alex first? I might punch MorganElla in the face if I thought it would stop her from Fotobombing me.

"This isn't funny to me either! I was fine in Virginia! And we'd still be there if Kiera hadn't bullied . . ."

And that's when they see me.

"Why are *you* here?" Alex asks in a not-very-nice way.

"Manners," Mr. Ray chides.

"Dad," Alex grumbles. "She just walked into our house uninvited . . ."

"Kaytee and her mother aren't home right now," Mr. Ray explains. "They're at the Villa Academy mother-daughter tea. Didn't she tell you?"

Alex is giving me the dirtiest look. I have no idea what I did to make him so angry, but I don't want to stick around long enough to find out.

"Nuuuh . . ."

It's all I can grunt before scuttling out the door. Alex's unfinished sentence echoes in my ears. An unanswered question echoes in my head:

Who is Kiera? And did she bully Kaytee so badly her family had to move? Is a shared history of mean girl abuse why we got along so well from the start?

I race home to my laptop and immediately Google "Kiera" and "Virginia."

Over nine million results. None of which get me any closer to identifying the source of Kaytee's secret torment. Maybe I'll do better if I Google "Kaytee Ray" instead?

This time I get nothing. Absolutely nothing.

It's as if Kaytee Ray did not exist before her family moved to New Jersey.

Does her family's strict no-social-media policy also apply to her twin?

I Google "Alex Ray" and "Virginia."

There's a bunch of hits, mostly soccer stats. But nothing that resembles any "drama" that would result in him punching someone in the face. Didn't Kaytee play soccer too? Why would there be stats for him but not for her?

As a comparison, I do a search on myself.

"Sophie Dailey" and "New Jersey."

I don't expect a lot to pop up because I'm not allowed on the socials. But it's more info than Kaytee, less than Alex: a quote in a *Mercer County Observer* article about Girl Scouts volunteering for beach cleanup ("'Single-use plastics are choking our oceans,' said Sophie Dailey, 9, from Brownie Troop 196") and a reference in a PTO newsletter to my participation in the Shadybrook Elementary School Talent Show ("Sophie Dailey and Ella Plaza delighted the audience with a duet from *Wicked*"), for example. Just enough to prove that Sophie Dailey from New Jersey actually exists.

The absence of any online evidence of Kaytee's existence makes me uneasy. I don't know how to channel this anxious energy, so I go to the opposite end of the search engine optimization spectrum, where results are guaranteed. I search for "Morgan & Ella."

There are dozens of Morgan & Ella videos, so many more than the last time I surrendered to the same search. At first, they just sang together, but I guess they're trying to extend their brand, so they've crossed over into all standard influencer categories: room tours, hauls, makeovers, and so on. I only watch the singing videos. The singing videos are set up the same every time, with Morgan and Ella performing a duet in what I assume is Morgan's bedroom, but I don't know for sure because I've never been there. They cover pop songs mostly—Riley Quick and Kaytee K., of course, Ariana and Billie, Selena and Demi—though sometimes they'll sing songs from musicals.

Morgan and Ella are both sopranos. But there's room for only one lead vocalist in Morgan & Ella and that's Morgan. So Ella literally lowers herself to be the alto in the duo, always singing harmony, never the lead. When we sang together, I was the harmonizer but I preferred it that way. As Mrs. Mapleton used to tell me, "Melody is easy and gets all the attention. But harmony is harder, where the true beauty of the music is revealed."

That's the *second* most profound thing an adult has ever said to me.

Ella plays ukulele in every video. She taught herself by watching YouTube tutorials. This was one of the examples I'd use to make her feel better about being a different kind of smart. Ella isn't a prodigy or anything, but she's put in a lot of practice so she can handle basic arrangements and accompaniment. Morgan doesn't play any instruments, which is the only explanation I can think of for why she isn't a solo act.

Morgan & Ella averages about ten thousand views per video, which isn't a lot compared with the most popular YouTubers but is ten times more than the number of students who watched my duet with Ella at the fifth grade talent show. It's enough to make them minor celebrities who are asked to sing at ribbon cuttings, baseball games, and other local events. Second in popularity only to a Schuyler sisters' medley (18,247 views) is Morgan & Ella's cover of "Let It Go" (15,543), which speaks more to the unstoppable popularity of *Frozen* (and *Hamilton*) than Morgan & Ella's vocal skills.

I watch these Morgan & Ella videos

over

and over

and over

again.

I watch for a millionbilliontrillion forevers.

Or three hours to the rest of the world.

Let it go . . .

Let it go . . .

Let it go . . .

I watch and wonder how anyone could think Morgan & Ella sounds better than Ella and me.

I watch and I wonder if Kaytee would agree.

JUST LIKE PUKE

I'M GIVING "LET IT GO" ITS 15.558TH VIEW WHEN I HEAR MRS. RAY'S
car pulling into their driveway. I don't play it cool at all. I dash out
the door to greet them. To my shock, Kaytee is equally relieved to
see me. If not *more*.

"Sophie!" She clings to my arm. "You have no idea what I've
just been through!"

It's strange to catch Kaytee in her Villa Academy uniform. She
never lets me see her until she changes out of it. The khakis, green
polo, and gray cardigan aren't as "hideous," "ghastly," or "crimi-
nally fugly" as Kaytee described. But the outfit lacks Kaytee's
faboosh flair and she seems . . . well, like less of herself in it.

That's not the only difference in Kaytee's appearance. Her hair
is out of its ponytail and hanging in the kind of loose curls that
require a hot styling iron. In addition to her favorite lip gloss,
she's wearing what I think is mascara and maybe even eyeliner.

Overall, she appears less natural than normal. More done up. Still pretty, but it's closer to a trying-too-hard-like-Morgan kind of pretty that twists my insides.

"It wasn't that bad," says Mrs. Ray. She's in a red dress, a same-but-different version of the outfit she was wearing when we first met. She's got a bunch of dresses and heels she hardly gets to wear anymore since leaving her job in public relations. Right now Mrs. Ray is using her positive-spin skills to do damage control with her daughter.

"They were very gracious and welcoming," Kaytee's mom says now.

"And boring!" Kaytee replies. "I keep telling you those Villa Academy girls are totally stuck up and no fun at all! Just like Sophie says."

Mrs. Ray's eyes flit disapprovingly in my direction. I offer a weak smile.

"Kaytee, I'm disappointed in you," Mrs. Ray says wearily. "We talked about this. You promised not to judge someone before getting to know them . . ."

Kaytee is in no condition to listen to reason.

"It's been two whole weeks! I have gotten to know them! And I don't like them! The only thing worse than those girls is the uniform. Bleeeeeech! Green, gray, and beige! Green, gray, and beige! Just like puke!" She thrusts her wrist in my face. "And look, Sophie! My bracelet fell off this morning!"

"Enough with this nonsense about the bracelet."

Mrs. Ray looks and sounds exhausted.

"It's a sign!" Kaytee hops up and down. "The bracelet falling off is a sign that I'm not supposed to go there!" Kaytee spins around in a circle. "Villa Academy and me are not meant to be!" Kaytee flaps her arms above her head.

Usually I can't help but laugh whenever Kaytee goes all-out like this. But I'm too distracted by my frustratingly fruitless inquiry into Kiera from Virginia. Mrs. Ray is also not amused. At all. There is none of the mother-daughter chumminess I envy.

"Kaytee," she warns. "Settle down . . ."

"I can't settle down!" Kaytee cries out. "Not when you've put me in an unfashionable prison of plain, blah boringness!"

"Kaytee." Mrs. Ray isn't giving in to her daughter's dramatics. "We need to talk . . ."

"Can we talk about this later, Mom? Please? Pleeeeeeease?" Kaytee drops to her knees and grovels in the grass. "Sophie and I have to get out of here because we've wasted enough time today!"

"No, Kaytee," Mrs. Ray says firmly. "We need to talk about this right now. Say goodbye to Sophie."

Kaytee is stunned. Her charm offensives work so well on her mom. She isn't used to being rebuffed.

"But, Mom . . ."

Mrs. Ray has reached peak parental annoyance.

"Say goodbye to Sophie!"

Kaytee's whole body slumps as she marches wordlessly behind her mother.

First Alex wants me to go away.

And now Mrs. Ray does too.

Do they finally see through me?

Do they know I'm not who I say I am?

Do they know I've been lying to Kaytee from the moment we met?

WHATEVER WHAT?

THE LEMON HAS DRIED UP.

The battery lost its juice.

The clock slows down.

Every minute is an hour.

An hour is a day.

A day is a millionbilliontrillion forevers, as Kaytee would say.

I've forgotten how boring my life was before she moved next door. How lonely. I could get a fresh lemon, fix the clock, make time fly again. But it won't bring Kaytee here any quicker. I could get started on a new To Do. Number 16. Number 29. Number 33. It doesn't matter which one. They're all pointless without Kaytee.

Brainchatter rattles on and on.

Say goodbye to Sophie.

Let it go . . .

Say goodbye to Sophie.

Let it go . . .

Say goodbye to Sophie.

Let it go . . .

I wish I could ask Mom to make me a stomach-soothing mug of peppermint tea. But then she'll get all social-worky and want to know what's troubling me and I just can't have that conversation with her—with anyone—right now. It's much safer to stay upstairs in my room. Alone.

Alone.

Alone.

"Helloooooo, Sophie!"

Not alone!

I slam the laptop shut.

I'm brainchattering and tummyrumbling so hard about Kaytee's family catching on to my lies that I haven't even noticed her. I get like that sometimes. My parents call it The Zone, as in, "Watch out. Sophie's in The Zone again." It's not a good place to be. Not even the best breathing techniques or calming teas work when I'm in The Zone.

Kaytee jumps on my bed.

Kaytee jumps off my bed.

"What are you doing here?"

"What do you *mean* what am I doing here?"

She's out of the uniform, of course, and has changed into black leggings and a purple hoodie lit up by a rhinestone smiley face.

"Your mom was pretty upset," I say, "and didn't want you hanging out . . ."

With me.

"She's not happy about the truth," Kaytee says.

The truth . . . About me?

"Villa Academy is the worst."

I exhale for what feels like the first time in eleven-almost-twelve years. I still don't know what's going on with Alex, but maybe Mrs. Ray's bad mood has nothing to do with me after all?

"Is it really that bad?"

Kaytee clutches her chest like I do sometimes when heartpang is at its absolute worst. Is she about to tell me all about Kiera the Virginia Bully before I even have to ask?

"How can I possibly express my fabooshness in a *uniform*?"

Okay. I guess I can't blame her for not wanting to talk about her tormentor. I mean, I haven't exactly been up front with her about MorganElla. Maybe this is an opportunity for both of us to come clean. The empty Google searches reinforced how little I know about Kaytee's life in Virginia—problems or not. I've been too focused on avoiding conversations about my own "friends" to notice that Kaytee had been even tighter-lipped about hers. If only I hadn't lied in the first place. About MorganElla, or anything else. What will happen if she discovers the foundation of our friendship is a mountain of bullcrap?

"Did you eat lunch yet?"

I shake my head. Tummyrumble is crushing my appetite.

"Sweet! We can do number eleven!"

Kaytee has pretty much taken over the To Do List. She knows the book better than I do.

"Number eleven?"

"Try cuisine from another culture!"

My belly is still rebelling from stress. It's not an ideal time for foodie experimentation. But there's no way to change Kaytee's mind once she's gotten it fixed on a particular To Do. But maybe, just maybe, I can find a way to compromise.

"I think we've got some leftover Thai food in the fridge . . ."

"Leftover Thai food?" Kaytee blows air out her cheeks like *pfft*. "Even Nowheresville, Virginia, had Thai food. Today we're eating lunch at Whatever Wat!"

"Whatever *what*?"

"W-A-T, not W-H-A-T," Kaytee explains with a giggle. "It's the new Ethiopian restaurant in Stockton Square."

Stockton Square is the heart of our little downtown. I'm pretty sure Whatever Wat is located a few doors down from Frootie Smoothie. Even a House Two loser like me knows that's where all the House One girls hang out after school and on weekends.

"I'm sorry, Kaytee, but I can't go with you," I say. "I don't have any money."

She reaches into her back pocket and produces two crisp twenties.

"I've been saving up!" she says, fanning the twenty-dollar bills in front of her face. "My treat!"

"I don't want you to waste your money on me," I say. "I don't even know if I like Ethiopian food."

"Me neither! That's the whole point! And . . . well . . ."

She is having trouble looking me in the eye.

"What?"

"Aren't you bored just hanging out around here all the time?"

Translation: She's bored just hanging out around here all the time.

With me.

I know this because I've heard it before.

From Ella.

About me.

"Sophie? Are you okay? You look sick."

I feel sick.

"Come on, Ethiopian food can't be that bad."

It isn't Ethiopian food I'm worried about.

"I've always thought Sophie needed to develop a more adventurous palate," Dad says, pausing in front of my open bedroom door. "I think lunch at Whatever Wat is a wonderful idea."

"But, Dad," I begin. "I'm not sure there are vegetarian options on the menu."

"I already checked!" Kaytee says, looking very pleased with herself. "There are!"

Dad reaches into his pocket, takes out his wallet, and hands me a twenty.

"Just in case you want to go to the Creamery for cones afterward."

"Thank you, *Doctor* Dailey!"

My dad's eyes pop with pleasant surprise. Six years into our friendship and Ella would still insult my father by calling him "Mister" instead of "Doctor."

"Yeah," I mumble. "Thanks, Dad."

"Number eleven! Whee!"

"Number eleven. Whee."

Kaytee cracks up at my lack of enthusiasm. She thinks I'm being funny on purpose. But it isn't a laughing matter to me. Not at all.

"Come on," Kaytee says. "Let's go!"

I feel like I'm about to step onstage in front of a packed audience wearing nothing but my underwear. To perform a song I never learned how to sing.

Or couldn't even if I had.

THE DREADED INEVITABLE

ON THE TEN-MINUTE WALK DOWNTOWN, I THINK KAYTEE EXPLAINS that W-A-T is a traditional Ethiopian stew that's eaten by scooping it up with bread instead of spoons. And I think she riffs about the delicious efficiency of bread bowls in general, then follows it up with an unrelated tangent about clumsy penguins. But I can't be sure because the whole time she is talking and walking, I'm worrying about who we'll run into from Mercer Middle School.

We're within a block of our destination when the dreaded inevitable happens.

"Sophie!" Kaytee says, clutching my arm. "Aren't those your friends? The YouTubers? I love their cover of 'The Fullest Truth'!"

I guess I'm not the only one who watches Morgan & Ella's videos.

Morgan.

And.

Ella.

MorganElla.

And Maddy, of course. MorganElla doesn't go anywhere without a third girl to trail them in envy. Before Maddy, that third was Sofie-with-an-F, who came after Harumi. I wonder who will be next?

All three girls are wearing bedazzled hoodies and leggings. They've accessorized with oversized sunglasses and clutch colorful Frootie Smoothies in gigantic plastic cups. They look ridiculous to me, like aspiring reality TV housewives, but Kaytee's eyes are all lit up at the sight of them. I hate to admit it, but in her own bedazzled hoodie and leggings, she looks so much more like a faboosh girl who should be drinking Frootie Smoothies with them instead of eating weird foreign food with me.

"Come on! I want to meet all your other friends! Finally!"

All my other friends.

This is when the truth comes out about *all my other friends*.

This is when Kaytee discovers *all my other friends* don't exist.

This is when Kaytee asks all the dreaded inevitable questions and MorganElla provides all the dreaded inevitable answers.

This is when Kaytee learns what Alex and Mrs. Ray almost definitely already know and what she should have figured out long ago:

I have no other friends.

I am a liar.

Kaytee heads in their direction and I have no choice but to go with her.

Unless I turn and run the other way.

Kaytee grabs me by the arm.

"Let's go, Sophie!"

There is no escape. I feel my face turning the oceanic color on Kaytee's walls.

"Umm . . ."

MorganElla doesn't care about what I've been doing or where I've been. But she takes one look at Kaytee and is suddenly very, very interested in the company I've been keeping. This moment has potential to make fantastically mortifying Fotobomb material.

"Lookie who got a new BFF!"

Morgan's tone is high-fructose corn syrupy sweet.

"I'm Kaytee Ray! I spell it K-A-Y-T-E-E, just like Kaytee K.!" The words come bursting out of her mouth like she can't contain them for another second. "I loved your cover of 'The Fullest Truth'! I've seen all your videos! I love you!"

MorganElla has perfected her *aw shucks who me?* modesty face. It's a total act, just like Riley Quick whenever she wins an award.

"And we love you," MorganElla replies robotically.

Kaytee beams. "And you must be Maddy, right?"

Maddy blinks in shock. She can't believe Kaytee actually knows her name.

"I moved next door to Sophie this summer," Kaytee says. "I'm so happy to finally meet you all!"

"Ummm," says Morgan.

"Ohhkaaay," says Ella.

"Ummm, ohhkaaay," says Maddy.

It's still not too late to run away. Kaytee has let go of my arm, so I can flee the scene right now. Kaytee will still find out the truth about me, but I won't have to be around to watch it happen.

"I love your sunglasses!" Kaytee says to Morgan. "Where'd you get them?"

I see the sunglasses as Dad would: They are not polarizing and won't stop UVA and UVB exposure that can lead to cataracts, macular degeneration, and skin cancer.

"Oh, these?" Morgan nonanswers with a yawn.

"And those boots are so cute," she says to Ella. "I love the stacked heel."

Wearing heels causes a range of problems including bunions, ingrown toenails, and irreversible damage to leg tendons. It's easier to recall these facts than it is to focus on what's happening right in front of me.

"I know, right?" Ella says.

"And your hoodie is just the cutest," she says to Maddy.

Maddy is not used to such attention. She blushes.

Morgan lowers her sunglasses to get a better look at us. "So you must be in House Two."

"House? Two? Huh?" Kaytee asks, feigning confusion. "I'm in the house we moved into. Next door. To Sophie."

MorganElla rolls all four eyes.

Perhaps out of sympathy, Maddy explains, "She means House Two at Mercer?"

"I don't go to Mercer Middle," Kaytee grumbles. "I go to Villa Academy."

She turns to me with a perplexed look on her face. Why haven't I told them as much about her as I've told her about them? Morgan is gifted when it comes to girl-on-girl drama and immediately picks up on this tension.

RUN. RUN. RUUUUUUUUUN.

"Villa Academy. Well, that explains why I've never seen you before," Morgan says. "The girls there are totally stuck up."

"Yes!"

"And they don't have any boys or any decent clubs or anything."

"Yes!"

"I would *die* if I had to wear that uniform."

"YESSSSSSSSS!"

Kaytee's face is flooded with relief, like finally, *finally* someone gets it.

And that someone isn't me.

Kaytee is a millisecond away from impulsively pulling Morgan into a hug. But she's stopped by a sudden tectonic shift in energy. Morgan's eyebrows pop over her sunglasses and she clutches Ella's and Maddy's arms as if to stabilize herself.

"Omigoddess! It's *him*."

Ella fumbles her phone.

"Mystery hottie!" squeaks Maddy.

Kaytee and I turn to see the source of all the commotion.

"Ack." Kaytee gags. "That's my twin brother! And his friend!"

She's right, of course. Alex and another boy I've never seen before are kicking a soccer ball about a half block behind us. I'd say this afternoon can't possibly get any worse, but I'm tummy-rumbling so hard I might erupt right there on the sidewalk.

"The mystery hottie is your twin brother?"

Mystery hottie? Yuck. Now I'm *really* ready to explode. Dr. Dawson could discuss my death by spontaneous human combustion as part of our unit on chemical reactions.

"We've been wondering about him ever since he showed up around town last month," Maddy says. "Morgan's totally stalking him."

"I am not," Morgan snaps. "You're the one with zero chill, not me!"

Maddy looks like she wants to dive in and disappear into her bottomless smoothie.

"He goes to private school too," Kaytee explains. "Wilson Academy."

"He should totally transfer to Mercer!" Maddy says. "You'll make the cutest couple. I'm shipping you already!"

Morgan pretends to be bored by the conversation.

"What's his name anyway?" she asks in a totally offhand way.

"Alex," Kaytee answers.

"Alex! What should our ship name be?" Maddy wonders out loud. "Morgan. Alex. Morgan. Alex. MorLex?"

"Sounds like a laxative," Kaytee jokes. "That's perfect!"

If I weren't so nauseous, I'd laugh out loud. Maddy bites her lip. MorganElla doesn't crack a smile.

"Come onnnnn," Morgan says, yanking Kaytee's arm. "Let's say hi to your brother."

Now I'm forced to watch the flirtation between two people who hate me the most in the world. This is why I never go anywhere.

"The other boy is pretty cute too," Maddy says.

How can she even tell from this far away?

"Hey, Lexi!" Kaytee calls out. "You've got a fan club!"

"Lexi!" MorganElla and Maddy squeal. *"That's so cute!"*

"Lexi?" asks the other boy I don't know.

"I told you not to call me that!" Alex shouts back.

"He told you not to call him that!" MorganElla and Maddy giggle in a whiny babymonster way that many girls believe is attractive to boys. For all I know, maybe it *is* attractive to boys, though I can't understand why. At least flirting with the boys takes all the attention off me.

"I'm so sorry, *Alexander Michael Ray*," Kaytee says with sarcastic emphasis. "I'll never use the family nickname in public again."

"Morgan . . . Alexander . . ." Morgan says pensively. "XanGan?"

Alex grunts a hello. His friend bounces the ball on his head, which is just begging for a concussion. But that's the sort of dumb thing boys do in front of girls like MorganElla and Maddy. And I guess Kaytee too. He would not be showing off if it were just me. This I know.

"MorDer?" Ella suggests.

The friend stops inflicting brain damage on himself to flirt another way.

"'Morder' means 'to bite' in Spanish," he says. "Do you bite?"

Kaytee gags. Ella and Maddy giggle. Morgan reaches through the neck of her sweatshirt to adjust the shoulder straps on her bra. Now that I'm sort of developing, I can't ever imagine a scenario where I'd go out of my way to remind everyone about my boobs. I wonder how Kaytee will act when she gets them. Will she still be as shy about her body as she is now? Or will her show-offy side take over?

"Let's go, Diego."

Alex pulls his friend by the arm and drags him in the opposite direction.

"Byyyyyyyyyeeee, Alex!" MorganElla and Maddy singsong. "Byyyyyyyyyeeee, Diego!"

Middle school flirtation makes me superuncomfortable.

"You're the Mystery Hottie's sister!" Maddy gushes. "You're so lucky!"

"Ewww," Ella says. "You realize it would be, like, totally gross for Kaytee to have a crush on her own brother, right?"

"I didn't mean it that way!"

Morgan dismisses Maddy with the flick of her wrist.

"Well, if you and your brother ever decide to transfer to Mercer, be sure to ask for House One," she says. "That's the Cool House."

MorganElla and Maddy all point their index fingers in the air and make a little whooping sound that I guess is meant to signify their allegiance to the Cool House.

"Well," Kaytee says, glancing at me. "House Two is . . ."

Morgan will not waste precious time discussing the Uncool House.

"Oopsie! Gotta go! Sooo nice meeting you, Kaytee! Tell your brother we said heyyyyy." Then, the final blow. "Bye, Ickface."

MorganElla struts off and Maddy follows behind.

I've made it through the entire conversation without saying a word.

WHAT HAPPENS NEXT

I WANT KAYTEE TO ASK WHY MORGANELLA CALLED ME ICKFACE. Then I'll have a reason to let it all out. To finally tell her the truth. And then maybe that will inspire her to tell me the truth about Kiera the Virginia Bully.

But she doesn't ask.

"Morgan totally gets it! She understands why I hate Villa Academy! It's like I've been telling you all along, but you didn't believe me!"

"It's not that I didn't bel—"

Kaytee cuts me off.

"Morgan needs to come over and talk some sense into my mom!"

How did I not see this dreaded inevitable coming? A two-minute conversation is all it took for Morgan to become more valuable to Kaytee than I am.

"Your friends are fun."

She is wrong on both points.

They are not fun.

They are not my friends.

"But it was kind of weird though," Kaytee says. "I mean, why did Morgan and the other girls act like they'd never heard of me?"

What can I say to make sense of what just happened? If Kaytee is so willing to overlook Ickface, if she's so uninterested in the truth, then I need another lie. A new one. And lying is like any other skill, I guess. It gets easier with practice. Kind of like how I felt less and less guilty with every new delivery of Awkward Acquaintance Muffins.

"They know all about you," I say. "They're just jealous."

"Jealous?" Kaytee eyes me skeptically. "Why?"

"They're jealous because . . ."

Why? Why are they jealous?

"I told them I was inviting you to the beach house for a double birthday celebration and not them."

Yes! It's *definitely* getting easier to make stuff up as I go along. But it's all okay, right? As long as there's no harm done, right? And from the positively electric expression on Kaytee's face, I've done good here.

"Really?" Kaytee bounces up and down. "You picked me? Over them?"

"Yes!" I say. "Of course!"

Mom hasn't asked about my birthday since the first day of school. But I've overheard her saying things like "I'm worried about Sophie" and "I wonder why there isn't a single friend she wants to invite to the beach house" and "I wish I could get Ella out of that bad crowd and back into Sophie's life." My dad always replies with assurances like "Her grades are where they should be" and "I was a loner too" and "It's not your job to manage the social lives of middle schoolers." Inviting Kaytee will bring her great relief. Too many clients end up in her office because they spend too much time online and not enough building meaningful relationships in the real world.

"So you're all in for a double birthday sleepover at the beach house?"

A shadow passes over Kaytee's face, the enthusiastic spark snuffed out in an instant.

"A sleepover," she says quietly.

"Right, a sleepover," I say. "Saturday to Sunday. So do you want to come or not?"

The question hangs in the air.

And stays there.

Too long for the response to be what I want it to be.

"Ummm . . ."

It's not G3 below middle C. It's lower on the scale but close enough for my intestines to do double Dutch in the deepest part of my belly.

"Maybe," Kaytee says finally.

MorganElla strikes again. A two-minute conversation with the girlbeast and Kaytee's already avoiding me. We've arrived at Whatever Wat, but neither of us is up for trying cuisine from another culture.

"I've kind of lost my appetite," Kaytee says. "I'm sorry."

I'm relieved. My cramps are getting worse by the second. I just want to be alone.

Alone.

Alone.

"No harm done," I mumble, more to myself than to her. "No harm done."

Our conversation about Kiera will have to wait.

I race home and can't get to the bathroom fast enough. I don't have the urge to go number one or two, and I don't think I'm going to throw up, but I'm feeling so weirdly icky that the toilet feels like the safest place to be.

"How was Whatever Wat?"

"Not now, Dad!"

I push past him, slam the bathroom door behind me.

"I take it Ethiopian food doesn't agree with you, then?" Dad jokes from the other side.

I pull down my pants and nearly fall off the toilet seat.

"Get Mom!" I shout. "I need Mom!"

"I'm right here," Dad says. "What's wrong?"

"I need Mom," I say. "Get Mom!"

"Sophie! This isn't funny. What's going on?" Dad asks.

There's a red stain in my underwear.

"I think I just got my period."

I'd been lying about already getting it for so long that I kind of forgot that it would actually come. For real.

"I'll get your mother," says Dad without hesitation.

THE NEXT DAY

I'M DRAGGING THE RECYCLABLES TO THE CURB WHEN KAYTEE LEAPS off her porch and comes running straight at me, arms flung wide. I wonder if she can see how I've changed. I'm different today. I'm officially mature. My body is finally catching up with my brain.

"Yes!"

"Yes?"

"Yesssss! I'll sleep over!" she says. "I'll join you for a double birthday celebration!"

I wasn't expecting such a sudden and enthusiastic turnaround.

"Really?"

"Why do you sound so surprised?" she asks.

"It's just that, well, you didn't seem so excited about it when I asked," I say. "And you aren't known for holding back your excitement about anything."

"I'm sorry," she says. "I haven't slept over at anyone's house since . . ." She pauses. "Well, it's been a while. I wanted to make sure it was okay with my parents before I said yes."

Again, if I didn't know Kaytee's secret, her cautious response would seem out of character. The Kaytee I know says yes first and asks for permission later. But that's not who she was back in Virginia. I'll bet Kiera made sleepovers a nightmare. No wonder Kaytee hasn't had one in a long time.

"Are you up for number ninety-one?" Kaytee asks.

I'm more up to it today than I was yesterday. Mom rushed home to help me and rescue Dad. As much as my parents hate conforming to gender norms, Dad definitely didn't hesitate to pass the period responsibilities on to my mom. She showed me how to properly stick the pad so it would protect my underpants. She made peppermint tea that calmed my cramps. She took off her glasses, cupped my chin, and said, "You're not a little girl anymore."

"I can't think of a better way to spend a Sunday," I answer.

We spend the next hour or so going back and forth between our yards, foraging for long-stemmed daisies and ivy vines to weave into flower crowns. And the whole time we're at it, I'm bursting with my secret: *I'm not a little girl anymore!*

"I'm terrible at Skee-Ball," Kaytee says out of nowhere.

"It's all in the wrist," I tell her. "You can't let it go floppy . . ."

I mastered Skee-Ball at an old-timey arcade a few blocks away from the beach house. I'm so excited to take her there.

"I just hope it's still hot enough to swim!" Kaytee says.

I'm so glad my period will be over by then. I'm not ready for tampons and would've hated staying out of the water.

"Long-range weather forecasts aren't very accurate," I say, "but Dad says this September is trending warmer than average so . . ."

Kaytee pushes her sunglasses up on her nose. They're pink and way too big for her face.

Just like Morgan's.

"Getting 2 Hott N Herre," Kaytee sings terribly. *"Thirsty Earth gonna disappear . . ."*

If the weather cooperates, it will be easier to pretend that school hasn't started yet. It's technically still summer when we arrive at the beach house on my birthday, September twenty-second. It will officially be autumn when we return from the beach house on Kaytee's birthday, September twenty-third. Born one day apart and yet we're from different seasons. I'm trying not to think about the other differences.

Like her sunglasses.

Like my period.

"After today," she says, fanning herself with a fern frond, "you're more than halfway to getting a phone. With three months to go! Totally ahead of schedule!"

She's right. There aren't enough To Dos to stretch until January. Will Kaytee notice if we skip Impossible Number 45? Maybe I can tell her I already did it by myself? What's another little lie at this point . . . ?

"There's no guarantee we'll get them all done," I say.

"Of course we will!" she says. "Why wouldn't we—"

Her question gets cut off by a warrior scream.

"AAAAAAAAAAAAIIIIIIIIIIIIIIIIIIIIIIEEEEEEEEEEE . . ."

"Lexi! Watch out!"

"I TOLD YOU NOT TO CALL ME THAT!"

"Alex! Watch out!"

But Alex/Lexi doesn't watch out. Not at all. He tears right through the yard, runs right over all the clippings we've carefully laid out in the grass, reverses course, and tramples right over them a second time in the opposite direction just for jerky measure. It happens so fast, there's no time to even try to stop him, not that I could.

Kaytee doesn't seem bothered at all. She just rolls her eyes and sighs.

"I should've known better," she says. "The whole world is off-limits when Lexi—I mean, Alex—does his wind sprints."

I pick up a crushed buttercup and I swear I almost start to cry. I hate to admit when MorganElla is right about something, but I think my hormones are making me more emotional than usual. I mean, I know it's such a silly thing we're doing and yet it still matters. Actually, now more than ever before. The House Two teachers have been piling on the homework, making it tough to get together after school on most days. We see very little of each other lately so number 91 matters more to me than anything has mattered to me in a long time. Dad would call this a case of poorly ranked priorities, but I don't care.

It isn't right that we spent an hour getting all the right

blossoms and branches for all that work to be ruined by Alex's big, bully feet on one of only two days out of the whole week I shouldn't have to worry about bullies. It feels personal. And this time I can't keep my frustration to myself.

I'm not a little girl anymore.

"He's a jerk," I say. "By any name."

Kaytee bristles. "He's not always like this."

"He's *always* like this around me." I dig my heel into the crushed stems on the ground. "He's hated me from day one."

"Aw, come on," Kaytee says in a playful tone. "You're exaggerating."

"Fine," I snap back, unwilling to give in to her peacekeeping smile. "Alex liked the Awkward Acquaintance Muffins on day one, then started hating me on day two."

Kaytee gives me an amused, confused look.

"Awkward Acquaintance Muffins?"

"Forget I said that. That's got little to do with your brother hating me and trying to sabotage our friendship and you not doing anything to stop it."

I don't know how twins can be so different. It's as if all the words were divided between them when they were twinning together in Mrs. Ray's belly and Alex got five of them and Kaytee got all the rest. The phrases "hello, how are you?," "excuse me," and "sorry" are not in his repertoire when I'm around. And I tried so hard! I laughed when he farted and looked interested when he talked about his workouts and even tried to bribe him into liking me with batches of chocolate cupcakes that he allegedly loved, but

I had to take Kaytee's word for it because he never thanked me himself.

"I don't blame you for feeling this way," Kaytee says. "If I were you I'd take it personally too."

I used to wonder if I was a To Do on her private list: Keep an Ickface Company. Maybe it was an initiation rite, a prank Kaytee had to pull before acceptance into the Global Middle School Illuminati. Until I overheard Alex, I assumed Kaytee—pretty but not prissy, bubbly and bold in all the right ways—could make friends with anyone anywhere, anytime. As much as I hate that Kaytee was bullied in Virginia, I realize now that our shared outcast status is probably the only reason we're friends.

"He doesn't hate you," Kaytee says. "I swear."

Fine. Let's say Alex doesn't hate me. But he definitely doesn't *like* me. I don't get his attention the way girls like MorganElla and Maddy get his attention. I'm not sure if I even want boys to notice me. But it would be nice to have the option of not being ignored.

"Lexi is tough, but he's got a sweet side too," Kaytee continues. "A side that pets every puppy we pass on the street. The side that makes me stop whatever I'm doing, sit next to him on a bench, and admire a beautiful sunset. The side that lets me paint his toenails blue. The side that loves Riley Quick even though that's a totally dumb opinion because she is so obviously inferior to Kaytee K."

She's trying to make me laugh. It won't work today.

"I've never seen that side," I say simply.

"I know. But it's there."

Kaytee sees everyone's best side. She sees it in Alex. She thought she saw it in her brief meetup with MorganElla. I'm grateful she sees it in me too, especially when I have trouble seeing it myself.

CHALLENGES

MY DAD IS IN HIS OFFICE WEARING HIS NOISE-CANCELING headphones. Mrs. Ray and my mom are downstairs, supposedly discussing the details of the double birthday trip. They've never socialized before so I assumed they'd keep it all business—arrivals and departures and packing lists and whatnot. I hoped they'd keep it quick and to the point and avoid any conversation that might reveal me as the liar I am. But my mom opened a bottle of wine and it's turning into an embarrassing grown-up gigglefest. I always think it's weird when adults don't act their age, but now I've got reason to worry too.

Kaytee and I are upstairs. I finished my homework as soon as I got home, but Kaytee is just getting around to it now. Or not really because she's too busy clutching her stomach and rolling around on my floor to conjugate Spanish verbs.

"I'm staarrrrrrrrving."

"I'll get some snacks!"

This gives me an excuse to spy on our moms and make sure they stay on topic.

I slip downstairs to get a bag of sprouted bean crisps, which I've tried telling Kaytee taste a lot like potato chips if you've forgotten what potato chips taste like. This is easy for me because I haven't had real potato chips in fourteen months and six days.

My last sleepover at Ella's house.

I'm about halfway down the stairs when I catch part of the moms' conversation. Just as I had feared, the discussion has gone way off course.

"I practically forced Sophie to introduce herself to your daughter. I wish she were more social. I worry about her spending so much time by herself." Ice clinks in the glass. "What I'm trying to say is, Sophie is lucky to be Kaytee's friend."

This is all true.

And yet.

The way Mom is saying it . . .

Almost like she's apologizing.

Like she's embarrassed to be my mother.

Like she wishes she had another daughter.

One who is better at being the right kind of girl.

A girl who is pretty but not prissy.

Bubbly and bold in all the right ways.

All about seeing and doing and go go going!

A girl like Kaytee.

I sink to the floor. I don't want to hear any more, but I can't stop listening.

"The feeling is mutual," Mrs. Ray says. "I promise you."

A warm-and-fuzzy feeling washes over me. I know I'm lucky to be Kaytee's friend. But it's comforting to hear she's lucky to be mine too. The giddy lift lasts for about half a second before I'm flattened yet again.

"I'm surprised to hear you're worried about Sophie socially," Mrs. Ray says. "According to Kaytee, Sophie has a great group of girlfriends. They're in the popular squad? That's what they call it these days, right? A squad?"

I'm paralyzed in place.

"A *squad*?" My mother says the word as if she's trying out a foreign language. "Sophie hasn't mentioned anything about a *squad*."

"Really? Kaytee says they rule seventh grade," Mrs. Ray says. "That's why Kaytee was so surprised Sophie picked her to spend the weekend . . ."

RUMBLERUMBLERUMBLE . . .

"A *squad*?" Mom asks again.

"Kaytee talks about them all the time! Ella and Morgan the superstar singers. And Maddy the influencer genius."

CHATTERCHATTERCHATTER . . .

"I know Ella. But Morgan? Maddy?"

"Sophie's squad is one of the main reasons why Kaytee wants to transfer to Mercer Middle School. According to my daughter, the girls at Villa Academy are all so booooooooring compared with Sophie's squad."

PANGPANGPANG . . .

"Ella," Mom repeats. "Morgan? Maddy? Are you sure?"

RUMBLECHATTERPANGRUMBLECHATTERPANG RUMBLE

"SNEAK ATTACK!!!"

Kaytee grabs me by the shoulders and shakes me out of my full-on panic.

"What's taking you so long?" she asks.

I open my mouth and nothing comes out. Mom's voice shatters the silence.

"Kaytee wants to transfer? But she seems to be cruising right through this transition from childhood to teenhood without any problems at all . . ."

Kaytee's jaw drops.

"Cruising . . . right . . . through . . . ?" Mrs. Ray asks.

And then Mrs. Ray starts cackling as if Kaytee cruising through tweendom is the most preposterous thing anyone has ever said in all the history of moms gossiping over glasses of wine. Mrs. Ray's laugh is like Kaytee's crazy infectious laugh but even catchier, so I'm not surprised when my mom joins in even though she has no idea what she's laughing at exactly. In that way she reminds me of myself.

The weirdest thing is, Kaytee looks even more upset at her mom than I am at mine. She springs into action, pushes past me on the stairs, and sprints to the living room. It's Alex's life-or-death survival training put to immediate use.

"Moooom!" Kaytee screams. "Stop talking about my problems!"

Mrs. Ray is shocked by her daughter's outburst. My mom

puts on her neutral, professional, *I've-seen-and-heard-it-all* face.

"Kaytee," she says, visibly shaken. "I haven't said anything inappropriate. I was just telling Mrs. Dailey that all children have their challenges . . ."

"Moooooom. Stop! Just stop! I've been analyzed enough!"

And without another word, Kaytee marches out our front door. Mrs. Ray swiftly and apologetically follows after her daughter.

"Do you know what that was about?" Mom asks when it's all clear.

"No," I say. "I don't."

"Did Kaytee have social problems in Virginia?"

I know I'm supposed to go to a trusted adult with information like this. But it doesn't seem right for me to talk to Mom about Kaytee's mean girl trauma before I've discussed it with her myself. I try to act natural.

". . . No?"

My mother is *literally* an expert in adolescent behavior and sees right through my lie.

"Sophie! What aren't you telling me?"

"Nothing! I mean, *Alex* was the one with problems, not her."

"Hmm."

Mom takes her glasses off. Puts them back on. Removes them again.

"It's wonderful that you and Kaytee have gotten so close," she says, "and I'm even happier to hear you and Ella are spending time together again."

But . . . ?

"But has her bad crowd become your bad crowd?"

"What? No!"

Mom doesn't say anything. She keeps her eyes on me though, hoping I'll fill in the silence. This is one of the techniques she uses to get her clients talking. But she has no idea just how good I am at keeping quiet.

"Well," she says finally when I don't break. "I'd love to meet these girls."

"Who?"

"Your squad. All your other friends."

All my other friends.

"Morgan," Mom adds. "And Maddy."

I laugh. And it's not an amused laugh because "squad" sounds so corny coming out of Mom's mouth. I laugh a bitter laugh because I swear it's the first time Mom has ever so quickly and correctly remembered a non-client's name.

And now I have to lie to her too.

I tell Mom it's a shame the Prius only fits one person besides me in the back seat because I totally, totally 100 percent would have invited my whole awesome squad to join me for the double birthday weekend.

And she believes me. Despite the fact that she should know better.

Too many clients end up in her office because they are pathological liars out of touch with reality.

A WEEK OF QUESTIONS AND ANSWERS

"ARE YOU MAD AT ME FOR TAKING OFF THE OTHER NIGHT?" Kaytee asks.

"Is everything okay between you and Kaytee?" Mom asks.

"Is the squad still mad about your birthday?" Kaytee asks.

"Do you want to invite Ella, Morgan, or Maddy to join us?" Mom asks.

"Ummm . . . Why does your shirt look like it came out of a Dumpster?" Morgan asks.

"Can't you try just a *little* harder on your look?" Harumi asks.

"What do you know about Alex?" Maddy asks.

"Ummm . . . How is your hair limp and frizzy at the same time?" Morgan asks.

"Seriously, why don't we watch some beauty tutorials together?" Harumi asks.

"Why isn't Alex on Fotobomb?" Maddy asks.

"What are you doing for your birthday?" Sofie-with-an-F asks.

"Does Diego have a girlfriend?" Maddy asks.

"How did you do on the quiz on electricity and magnetism?" Dad asks.

"Why don't you raise your hand in my class, when I know you know the answers?" Dr. Dawson asks.

"Are you aware that class participation is twenty-five percent of your grade?" Señora Mar-TEEN asks.

"Why are you always over here?" Alex asks.

"Are you sure you don't want to invite Ella, Morgan, and Maddy?" Mom asks.

"Are you sure you want me instead of them?" Kaytee asks.

"Don't you have any other friends?" Alex asks.

"Ummm . . . Do you insist on walking down this hallway every day just to wreck my whole vibe with your pathetic aesthetic?" Morgan asks.

No. I hope so. Maybe. No. I don't know. I don't think so. Nothing. I don't know. I don't think so. I don't know. Nothing special. I don't know. A plus. I can't. Unfortunately, yes. I'm sorry. Yes. Yes. No. I . . . ?

"Are you looking forward to getting away this weekend?" I ask myself.

YES.

DOUBLE BIRTHDAY WEEKEND

AFTER THE LONGEST WEEK OF MY LIFE, IT'S FINALLY HERE!

Ocean temperatures might dip into the mid- to high-sixties, which is five to ten degrees lower than normal for this time of year. Dad can't resist explaining that this phenomenon is called "upwelling" and it's caused by heavy winds from the southwest pushing warm water away from the coastline and pulling cold water up from the ocean floor. It's not ideal beach weather for our double birthday celebration but we decide to make the best of it, which isn't hard to do when I'm with Kaytee far, far away from Mercer Middle School.

"Thanks a lot, global warming!" Kaytee replies sarcastically from the back seat.

Dad shoots me a look in the rearview. I know what he's thinking. Climate change is not a laughing matter because making jokes minimizes the urgency to reverse the disastrous impact greenhouse gases are having on our environment. But I don't let his glance get me down. I'm too happy. I've been looking forward to this trip all week. Having just a little bit of hope helped me cope with MorganElla's daily shaming in the Hallway of Doom. At least the ummms and Fotobombs, LOLZ and EWWZ, are predictable. It's the unknown dreaded inevitables that are tougher to deal with. Like what will happen if—when—Kaytee runs into them again.

This weekend we're 125 miles away from Frootie Smoothie.

For two days I am safe.

"Mom, thanks again for working out all the details with Mrs. Ray!"

My mom turns around in the passenger side and smiles at us.

"It's a pleasure," she says.

"And thanks for driving, Dad."

Dad clears his throat. At this point he doesn't have anything against Kaytee personally, but he still blames her parents for her lack of serious concern for environmental matters. The ride is an opportunity to deprogram and rehabilitate.

"Girls."

And then he launches into a lecture about how carbon dioxide in the air is absorbed by the ocean, which leads to a drop in pH levels and acidification and lots of other dire consequences for marine life.

"Don't worry," I confide in Kaytee's ear, "I think dolphins are immune."

And we giggle at that and just about everything else my parents have to say for the next hour and twenty minutes. I've spent all my birthdays at the beach house, but I can't remember ever being this excited before. I can't wait to share my traditions with Kaytee. My two worlds are closing in on each other. It's a catastrophic collision course with Kaytee on one side, MorganElla on the other, and me in the middle. But the cataclysm won't happen today. Or tomorrow.

And that alone is reason to celebrate.

"We always go on the Double Trouble coaster first. And we have to blow out the candles on a birthday funnel cake! With rainbow sprinkles! I'll get mine today and you'll get yours tomorrow! It's mandatory!"

My parents veto fried, sugary foods but make an exception on my birthday.

"We have to get a picture in front of Riley Quick's house," Kaytee says.

"You're betraying the Kayters to become a Ribot?"

I flop over in a pretend faint. Kaytee shakes me awake.

"Never! How disloyal do you think I am? The photo is for Lexi. Tomorrow is his birthday too."

Ugh. I slump again, this time for real.

"Right," I say, "he's a secret Riley Quick fan."

"Lexi and I have never been apart on our birthday before," Kaytee says. "Before I left for the beach, he was all worried how being separated might bring his team bad luck in his soccer tournament. Because any change in the routine could wreck a whole season."

"Alex is superstitious?"

I find this hard to believe. I try to imagine Alex sitting beside us on Kaytee's floor, discussing horoscopes, making worry dolls, and designing dream catchers.

"Totally! Especially when it comes to sports. Last year his team was on a winning streak so he kept wearing the same pair of underwear and wouldn't let my mom wash them!"

"Ack! Boys are so gross!"

Kaytee agrees. "Totally."

When we pull up in front of the beach house, Kaytee springs herself from her seat belt before the car has come to a full stop. She doesn't want to waste a single second of sun.

"Beach! Beach! Beach!" Kaytee pumps her fist.

"Beach! Beach! Beach!" I pump my fist like Kaytee.

My parents haven't even gotten out of the car and Kaytee is already stripping off her T-shirt and kicking off her shorts.

"Woo-hoo! Let's go!"

We're both wearing our swimsuits under our clothes. Kaytee's is a polka-dot tank with a little skirt that's intentionally retro in a way I recognize immediately.

"Just like Kaytee K.'s suit in the 'Herstory' video!" I say.

When Kaytee takes a bow, I notice the "Herstory" suit comes with a little extra padding built into the bust. It's not enough to give her massive cleavage, but for the first time ever she looks as developed as I do in my black racer-back one-piece. It clings like skin on a seal.

"Can we go?" I ask. "The lifeguards are on duty."

"Not without an adult," Mom says. "Kaytee is our responsibility."

"We have to unpack the car fir—"

And the sentence isn't even out of Dad's mouth before Kaytee is grabbing as much as she can out of the trunk.

"Come on, Sophie!" she says. "The more bags we carry, the quicker we'll be unpacked and the sooner we can get to the beach!"

My parents exchange impressed looks.

The Prius is a pretty small car so it takes less than five minutes to unload. Mom is willing to stay behind to put away all the groceries so my Dad offers to take us to the beach. I swear Kaytee might burst into flames when my parents tell me I have to reapply my waterproof sunblock before I even think about swimming.

"We need to get our chairs, our towels, our . . ."

"Beach! Beach! Beach!" Kaytee chants.

Even my Dad can't resist Kaytee's gusto.

"Okay," he says, pumping his fist in the air. "Beach, beach, beach."

We start down the sidewalk in sort of a trot, but Kaytee picks up the pace as we get closer to the water. We zip past the lifeguard stand in a full sprint. I stop at the water's edge to test the temperature with my toe. Kaytee dives right in.

I'm looking forward to singing "Happy Birthday" to myself tonight and Kaytee tomorrow. Loudly, proudly, and beautifully, just like Mrs. Mapleton used to encourage me to. And maybe, just maybe, I'll follow it up with "Oh Oh Ocean" and "The Fullest Truth." And as a grand finale . . . number 45! That's right! I'm feeling brave enough to conquer number 45, the one I'd avoided because it felt—unlike all the others—impossible.

Today—one hour and twenty-five minutes away from MorganElla—it doesn't feel that way.

I'm wearing my birthday present from Kaytee: a pink-and-purple-striped hoodie decorated with a rhinestone two-fingered peace sign. According to Kaytee, peace signs are on trend. She was so eager to see me in it that I popped it right over my swimsuit when it got breezy on the beach. It's something she'd wear, or MorganElla. This isn't necessarily bad, but I can't help but wonder if Kaytee bought it because she thought *I'd* like it or because *she* did. She's always admired my Eco/Echo shirts—the same ones MorganElla compares to moldy cheese and garbage—so I'm giving her the most colorful design from their collection: a sunset swirl of pink, purple, and orange.

I wonder if her friends from Virginia—Allie? Gracie?—have put as much thought into her gift as I have. She's been gone for less than three months. Surely her besties will go out of their way to make her feel special, even from 250 miles away . . . right?

Unless Kiera has pressured them into ignoring her altogether . . . ?

"Come on in! The water's fine!"

It's hard to believe that someone as exuberant and independent as Kaytee could be intimidated by anyone.

"It's freezing!" I shout. "You must be an Arctic dolphin!"

"I'm the rarest of specimens!" Kaytee hollers to the sky.

Kaytee looks happier than ever. If I wouldn't miss her so much, I'd encourage her to lead the dolphin clique and swim on forever.

PART THREE

PAIRING UP

THE DOUBLE BIRTHDAY WEEKEND COULDN'T HAVE BEEN MORE FUN!
Kaytee and I splashed in the waves and cartwheeled across the sand
and raced hermit crabs and played impossible-to-win boardwalk
games for cheesy stuffed animal prizes.

I wish I were still at the beach with Kaytee instead of in the
bleachers with Harumi and Sofie-with-an-F waiting for another
terrible phys ed class to begin. Ella slinks into the gym late as usual,
and I can't help but notice she looks even more miserable than
I do. I tug at the pink-on-pink-on-six-different-pinks friendship
bracelet Kaytee made me right after we first met. I count backward. Eight weeks. We've known each other for eight weeks. I was
best friends with Ella for six years and I never felt as connected
to her as I do to Kaytee.

Coach Stout marches to center court and blows a whistle to
get our attention.

"It's that time of year again!" She pumps her fists. "Physical fitness testing!"

Everyone groans. No one louder than me. I'm usually confident about my test-taking ability, but this yearly check on my lack of athleticism is always a major low point for me.

Coach blows a whistle to quiet us down.

"Pair up!"

Harumi and Sofie-with-an-F break the world record for partner picking. I've never seen anyone move so fast! I'm wondering if Coach will let the three of us work together when she points a finger at Ella, then at me.

"You two. Pair up!"

Ella is obviously the last person in this gym I want to pair up with. And I'm sure she feels the same way about me. But even in moments of pure dread, my instincts won't allow me to disobey authority. I drag myself over to an open spot on the mat because we're starting with sit-ups. Coach instructs us to take turns to see how many we can do in sixty seconds. One holds feet and counts, the other crunches. Then switch.

"Do you want to go?" Ella asks. "Or should I?"

These are the first one-on-one words she's spoken to me in over a year.

"I don't want to do this at all," I mumble.

Ella's sneakers look brand-new, but I know the dirty truth. Even "spotless" shoes are swarming with nasty bacteria.

"This is very unsanitary," I say.

I try to make as little contact with Ella's sneakers as physically possible.

Just like Ella avoids me, I think as Coach Stout blows the whistle.

Ella completes thirty-five crunches in a minute. She comes up halfway on the last one and if we were still best friends, I might've considered giving her credit for thirty-six even if she hadn't totally earned it.

But we aren't.

So I don't.

We don't say anything when we swap spots on the mat.

I already rely on deep breathing to alleviate anxiety. But proper respiration techniques are a crucial part of exercising safely and efficiently. It's obvious, but fueling muscles with oxygen isn't something I'd given much thought to until *The Book of Awesome for Awesome Girls* number 9: "Practice Yoga and Mindful Breathwork."

Crunch, exhale.

"WHOOSH!"

Uncrunch, inhale.

"SHOOHW!"

Crunch, exhale.

"WHOOSH!"

Uncrunch, inhale.

"SHOOHW!"

I do this over and over again, fast at first.

"WHOOSH!"

"SHOOHW!"

"WHOOSH!"

"SHOOHW!"

But as the seconds tick away, my midsection begins to burn and I slow down a lot.

"WHOOSH . . ."

. . .

. . .

"SHOOHW . . ."

With five seconds left, I'm on crunch thirty-four . . . thirty-five . . .

"Come on, Sophie!" Ella cheers. "You can do it!"

The whistle blows as I fall back with a final "SHOOOOOOOOOOOOOHW!"

"Thirty-six!" Ella whoops. "One more than me!"

I've earned it. This isn't a favor between ex–best friends. And yet Ella's pretty face is all lit up like she's genuinely happy for me.

"I didn't think I could do so many," I confess.

"Oh, I knew you could do it," Ella says. "You *were* the underwater karaoke champ."

So Ella *does* remember the fun we used to have at the pool together. I'm stunned to hear her acknowledge the memory out loud. What if someone overhears and reports back to Morgan? Maybe Ella doesn't care?

"Next up! Flexibility testing!" shouts Coach Stout.

This won't be as exhausting as the crunches. We just sit and stretch our arms out in front of us as far as we can reach.

"Oh, I like this one," Ella says. "With my monkey arms, I've got an advantage."

I know Ella is only being nice to me because Morgan isn't around. And there's a very good chance she'll go right back to Fotobombing me when gym is over. But I've missed our friendship so much that I want this positive moment to last as long as possible. I slip back into the role of reassuring friend with ease.

"Lauren only said you had monkey arms to torture you," I say. "I'll never understand why siblings bully one another like that. You should see the battles Kaytee and Alex get into!"

We lower ourselves to the mat. Stretching our legs out in front of us, I close my eyes and imagine we're side by side on beach towels in the shade, swapping damp copies of *The Dragonologist Chronicles* . . .

I wonder if Ella has gotten rid of all her books.

I wonder if Kaytee would play underwater karaoke.

I wonder if Ella would like Kaytee.

I wonder if Kaytee would like Ella.

I wonder if Kaytee would like Ella more than she likes me.

"You must be so happy about the news," Ella says.

"What news?" I ask cautiously.

"The news," she says, "about Kaytee."

The mind/body rebellion is instantaneous.

RUMBLE.

CHATTER.

PANG.

"Kaytee," Ella continues, "is leaving Villa Academy and coming to Mercer."

RUMBLECHATTERPANGRUMBLERUMBLE
CHATTERPANGRUMBLE

I can barely force the words out of my mouth.

"How do you know this?"

Ella winces at my question as if the answer is as shocking and painful to her as it will be to me. Which in no way can possibly be true.

"I guess she's been messaging Morgan and . . ."

I double over in intestine-twisting torment at the incredible truth:

Morgan Middleton is stealing my best friend.

Again.

Why are my best friends so easily stolen?

Ella hovers over me, unable—or unwilling—to offer any words of consolation.

Coach Stout blows the whistle.

"Next up! Chin-ups!"

Ella kind of nudges me toward the horizontal bars. This is as close as I'll get to a comforting gesture from this person I've hugged hundreds, no, *thousands*, of times.

I barely grip the bar before letting go.

I limp the shuttle run.

I lie down for push-ups.

For the first time in my life, I fail on purpose.

BEST WORST NEWS

I'M BUMPITY-BUMP-BUMPED OUT OF SLEEP BY KAYTEE JUMPING UP and down on my bed.

"Wake up!"

I'm totally disoriented. What time is it? What *day* is it?

"Wake up! Up! Uuuuuuuup!"

I clip Kaytee's leg and she falls face-first onto the mattress. I guess I've picked up a thing or two watching Kaytee and Alex battle.

"I've got the best news!"

"Huh?" I mutter groggily. "What?"

Kaytee's words come out in a rush.

"I wanted to tell you in Pebble Harbor, but it took forever for my parents to work out the details and I didn't know for sure until this morning so this is kind of like a belated birthday present . . ."

"But you already gave me a present . . ." I mumble, still more asleep than awake.

I'd worn the peace sign hoodie to school. It's something MorganElla would wear, so how could she mock me for it? I thought I was Fotobomb-proof. Maybe for the first time ever I could get a GOALZ instead of LOLZ or EWWZ.

I underestimated MorganElla's evil genius.

"Ummm . . . The clearance rack wants its bargain back!"

"Is tryhard one word or two?"

It's this half-awake memory of the girlbeast's latest torture technique that jolts me to full consciousness.

Morgan is stealing my best friend.

And Kaytee is letting herself be stolen.

I get so caught up in the awfulness of this reality that I miss Kaytee's major announcement.

"Sophie! Did you hear me?" She bounces on the bed three times, flips in the air, and flops down beside me. "I'm transferring to Mercer Middle School!"

So what Ella told me is true. Which means it must also be true that Kaytee shared this news with Morgan before she shared it with me.

"I'm transferring to Mercer Middle School!" She's kicking her legs in the air because she can't contain herself. "I talked my parents into it!"

In my daze, Kaytee gives me a lot of information at once. The girls at Villa Academy are boring at best and snooty at worst. And I've made my life with *all my other friends* at Mercer sound so awesome, no wonder Kaytee made it her mission to get in on all the fun. And I guess my parents raved to hers about the excellent public schools and the highly ranked junior high in particular and, well, here we are.

"We're going to the same school!"

She's jumping up and down on my bed again.

This is the best news.

This is the worst news.

This is the best worst news.

And she broke it to Morgan before me.

Kaytee takes a step backward, almost off the edge of the bed.

"What's wrong with you?" she asks. "Why do you look like you just got a whiff of one of Lexi's ripest farts?"

"I . . ."

I don't know what to say. Do I let on that I already knew? Do I confront her about telling Morgan first? Do I ask why my best friends find me so easily ditchable? Do I ask her what Kiera did to her in Virginia?

"I deliver the best news ever, and you're turning it into a major downer. If I didn't know any better, I'd think you didn't want me to go to the same school as you."

My face betrays me. Kaytee blinks hard and rubs her eyes as if she can't believe what she's just seen.

"You *don't* want us to go to the same school?"

"I didn't say that."

Kaytee thrusts her chin at me and dips her hip defiantly.

"I don't hear you *not* saying it either."

"It's just . . ."

I can't look at her as I struggle to find the right words. I focus on the friendship bracelet on my wrist. The palest pink thread has gotten a bit dingy in the past week or so.

Kaytee snaps her fingers in my face.

"Don't pull the silent treatment with me! Talk to me! Tell me what's going on!"

"It's just . . ." I begin again. "I'm not sure Mercer is the right school for you . . ."

Kaytee's face goes slack. And we just stand there for a few seconds, both of us mustering the courage to say what needs to be said next. It's no surprise when Kaytee breaks the standoff.

"Stop the excuses," Kaytee says. "You obviously don't want to be seen with me."

"No! That's not true!"

"You think I'm not good enough for you and your pretty, perfect, popular friends. That's why you kept me away from them since I moved here. You're embarrassed of me!"

I never wanted Kaytee to think I'm embarrassed of her!

"Kaytee! Calm down! I didn't introduce you to Morgan, Ella, and Maddy because . . ."

I didn't want her to know I was embarrassed of myself.

"I didn't want to make you jealous," I say instead. "Because I knew it might be hard for you to find a tight group of friends at Villa Academy."

Why am I still perpetuating this lie? MorganElla is not my friend. I don't have any friends. Not real friends. Not like her. And once she starts at Mercer and she sees what MorganElla really thinks of me, I won't have her anymore either. I could've maybe gotten away with this charade if Kaytee stayed far away from Mercer Middle. But now? No way.

"Your friends are my friends!" Kaytee whoops.

Wait . . . Did I hear that right?

I'd never considered that Kaytee would see it that way. Is that why she told Morgan before me? If I had a phone, would Kaytee have messaged *me* and not Morgan? Or maybe it's possible Kaytee wanted to tell me in person because I'm more important than Morgan?

My friends are Kaytee's friends.

I try to picture what this might look like.

I see us walking into Mercer together. I see us slipping silly notes into lockers and studying for tests and partnering up on projects. I see us eating lunch with Harumi and Sofie-with-an-F.

My chest is pounding, but it's not heartpang.

My belly is fluttering, but it's not tummyrumble.

My mind is racing, but it's not brainchatter.

I'm feeling . . . excited? Like this could actually happen?

The optimism created by my positive visualization exercise doesn't last very long. My imagination can't compete with reality.

"I only wish . . ." Kaytee's next words come out slowly, ". . . they put me in House Two. With you."

She holds up her index finger and makes the whooping sound.

And that's when I realize that there is a fate far worse than me being in the same House as MorganElla.

It's Kaytee.

In the Cool House.

With MorganElla.

Without me.

Did she ask for it, like Morgan told her to do? Because Morgan "totally gets it" in a way I never did? Will being in the Cool House stop whatever bad stuff went down in Virginia from happening again here?

Inhale.

Expand the belly.

Count to three.

Exhale.

Squeeze the belly.

Count to three.

"Even if we don't have any classes together," she says, "we can still work on the To Dos after school and on weekends, right? You were my first friend in New Jersey. I'll never forget that."

She holds out her pinkie. I hook mine around hers, and we shake.

I know Kaytee wants it to be true. She believes it's possible. But she doesn't know MorganElla like I do. And desperate times call for desperate measures.

"There's something you need to know about me and my friends."

WHAT I SHOULD TELL KAYTEE

I USED TO SING.

I used to sing with Ella.

We'd draw pictures of butterflies and sing. We'd bake cookies and sing. We'd soar on the swings and sing. We'd plunge underwater and sing. On car rides to and from Girl Scouts, we'd sing along to the radio—she took the high parts and I took the low—and our voices blended beautifully.

We turned any solo into a duet.

I miss singing.

I miss Mrs. Mapleton too.

But I miss Ella the most.

The old Ella though. The way she used to be.

She was my best friend from the first day of kindergarten through the first day of sixth grade. But she morphed into half the girlbeast and it doesn't even seem worthwhile to talk about the friendship we used to have. Maybe we'd still be friends if Morgan hadn't so easily convinced Ella to sing with her instead.

This is how sixth grade *really* began.

In all my years at Shadybrook, I had managed not to be in the same class with Morgan. I knew who she was, of course, everyone did. I'd had enough solos in choir for her to at least know my name, but she had never spoken to me. I was flabbergasted when she complimented me on the first day of our final year of elementary school.

"I like your shirt, Sophie."

I almost fell over. Morgan knew who I was? MORGAN KNEW WHO I WAS.

"Oh, wow!" I beamed with pride. "Thank you, Morgan!"

"Ummm . . . I was talking to So*fffff*ie."

She spit the consonant at me as if I were so stupid to not hear the difference between *ph* and *f* out loud. And why wouldn't she question my intelligence? After all, I *was* stupid enough to think Morgan would be impressed by a Dragonologist Chronicles tee.

Morgan was the sun around which Ella and five other girls in Miss Chen's class—Sofie-with-an-F, Other-Sophie-with-a-PH, Maddy, Harumi, and Olivia—revolved. Within a week, Morgan was calling me Ickface, to let me, Ella, and everyone else know that I was way, way out of her orbit. I was the ex-planet formerly known as Pluto.

I've been exiled to the farthest outskirts of girl universe ever since.

Unfortunately, that still isn't far enough away to stop my world from collapsing in on itself.

WHAT I TELL HER INSTEAD

"MORGAN. ELLA. AND I HAD A MAJOR FALLING-OUT."

"You did?" Kaytee gasps. "About taking me to the beach house?"

She's so upset, I almost take it back.

Almost.

"It started with that," I say, making it all up as I go. "But got way worse."

"Over what?"

"Over . . ."

Even an Uncool House nonparticipant like me knows the greatest source of girl-against-girl drama.

"A boy."

"A *boy*?"

It sounds ridiculous because it is.

"Over . . ." Even after all the lies I've told, I still can't believe I'm going to say what I'm about to say. "Alex."

"Alex?" Kaytee blinks hard. "As in my twin brother, Alex?"

"Yes," I say.

And then I hear myself telling her how Morgan accused me of flirting with him just because I knew she liked him and now she's not talking to me anymore, which means Ella and Maddy aren't talking to me anymore either.

"She thinks you violated sacred girl code," Kaytee says. "Besties over all the resties."

I'm pretty sure that motto is from a Kaytee K. song, but I don't have time to ask.

"But that's totally stupid," Kaytee says, "because you hate Alex."

"And he hates me."

She doesn't deny it.

"Why didn't you say anything about this sooner?"

"I didn't want you to get caught up in all the drama."

But Kaytee isn't at all put off by all the drama. She's excited about it.

"I'm totally taking your side," she says. "This is *exactly* the sort of fun I've been missing out on at boring Villa Academy!"

Fun? How is this fun? My bogusness has totally backfired. Kaytee is more eager than ever to get started at Mercer.

"Don't be surprised if Morgan and Ella and Maddy pretend I don't exist," I say, scrambling to salvage the situation. "Just like they pretended they had no idea who you were when they met you."

Kaytee strikes a champion's pose.

"I'll never be friends with anyone who would treat you like that!"

"Morgan can be very persuasive . . ."

"Oh, *whatever*," Kaytee says, tossing her hair over her shoulder. "It's not going to work on me. I will never, ever be besties with Morgan."

Could it *really* be this easy to keep them away from each other?

"Promise?" I ask.

Her expression dims.

"Sophie," she says in a serious tone. "You're my first friend in New Jersey. I won't forget you. I'd *never* choose those other girls over you."

Even though I know I'm asking for the impossible, I can't help myself from asking again.

"Promise?"

"Promise!" The razzle-dazzle returns to her face. "They can't intimidate me. I am amazing, krazing, blazing . . ."

Sometimes it's tough to keep up with the theatrics that play across her expressive features. It can be almost too much to take in at such close range. Kaytee is meant for the stage. Kaytee plays all the way to the back rows. She's going to be a smash hit at Mercer Middle School. I just know it.

It's a dreaded inevitable.

BEST WORST DAY

TODAY MY BFF STARTS MERCER MIDDLE SCHOOL.

It is the best day.

It is the worst day.

It's the best worst day of my life.

Kaytee has not stopped chattering since she pirouetted onto my front porch this morning.

"I want to be cute but not like a tryhard." She twirls to show off her outfit: black skinny jeans and a white fitted tee scattered with silver polka dots. "I'm paranoid that a month of uniforms destroyed my fashion sense."

I'd hoped that she might wear the Eco/Echo shirt I gave her on her birthday, but she opted for this look instead. The outfit is, of course, perfect. It looks just like something MorganElla would wear. I give her a thumbs-up.

"My shirt is so cute on you," Kaytee says, skipping down the sidewalk.

Yesterday when Kaytee was choosing a First Day at Mercer outfit, she caught me inspecting an aqua T-shirt with an embellished pocket and trim. I was checking the label to see if the shirt was made in the USA or at an overseas factory that relies on child labor to keep costs down and profits up. She misinterpreted my interest and insisted I wear it to school today.

"You can borrow anything of mine anytime!"

I nod and resist the urge to scratch at the sequins scraping my neck.

"So was House One always the Cool House?" Kaytee asks.

"I don't know," I say.

"Maybe it's because the number one comes before two and is automatically ranked higher or something?"

"I don't know," I say.

"Do you think House Two can ever get its coolness back?"

Not if it's up to Ickface, Chewy, and Lickity Lick.

"I don't know," I say.

Kaytee stops walking and talking. She grips my shoulders.

"You need to stop worrying about me," she says. "I'll handle those girls just fine."

It's not Kaytee I'm worried about. And within seconds of hitting the school grounds, my instincts are proven right. All heads turn as Kaytee and I walk through the entrance together. The arrival of such an approachable pretty new girl does not go unnoticed.

"*Who is she?*"

"*Have you ever seen her before?*"

"*What's she doing here?*"

Kaytee doesn't shrink under the scrutiny. She . . . shines. Just like her radiant last name.

"This is going to be the best!"

Kaytee squeals, gives me a quick hug, and rushes down the hall toward homeroom.

It almost feels like I'll never see her again.

It almost feels like it would be easier that way.

SCHOOLED

THROUGHOUT THE DAY I CATCH MANY GLIMPSES OF KAYTEE'S LIFE at Mercer Middle School without me. I see for myself how she handles MorganElla just fine.

Better than fine.

They make a whole new hallway formation, a powerful one, with Morgan and Ella flanking her on either side and Maddy behind. It's clear they are following her and not vice versa. I'm actually kind of proud of her, in a way, considering what she's had to overcome. If only Kiera could see her now! Kaytee never looks lost, alone, or unhappy. Kaytee looks like she belongs. I know the same can't be said for me, except when Kaytee generously calls out to me, going out of her way to prove she's making good on her promise.

Outside the art room:

"Sophie! My locker!"

Outside the gym:

"Sophie! My social studies teacher!"

Outside the cafeteria:

"Sophie! I so seriously love that shirt on you!"

By this point, the embellished collar has given me a rash on my neck. Perfect Fotobomb material.

"Ummm . . ." Morgan pulls out her phone. "She's, like, *literally* allergic to cuteness."

Ella and Maddy laugh like they always do. Kaytee does not. She gives MorganElla IMAX-level side-eye.

"Not funny."

Morgan quickly puts her phone away.

Kaytee grins and waves goodbye at me.

"See you later, Sophie!"

Like all hallway drama, it only lasts a few seconds. But Kaytee's impact on the seventh grade social dynamic at Mercer Middle School is immediate and major.

"Did you *see* that?" marvels Harumi. "Morgan got schooled by the new girl."

"Who is she anyway?" Sofie-with-an-F asks.

For the first time in my middle school life, I have valuable information worth sharing. It's an unfamiliar feeling, but one I'd enjoy getting used to.

Power.

"That's Kaytee," I reply. "The girl who moved in next door to me over the summer."

"I thought you said she went to Villa Academy," Sofie-with-an-F says.

"Why is she here now?" Harumi asks.

"She transferred to be with me." Then, because I can't resist, I add, "Because I'm her best friend."

I don't mean to sound like I'm bragging, but it definitely comes out that way.

Harumi and Sofie-with-an-F exchange surprised looks. I don't have to ask why this is so difficult for them to believe. But still, it stings.

"Really?" Sofie-with-an-F asks.

"Yes, really," I reply. "We have a lot in common."

"Sure," Harumi says. "But for how long?"

Harumi and Sofie-with-an-F make the worst squad ever. They're too truthful to be unconditionally supportive. Say what you want about MorganElla and Maddy, but at least they're loyal to each other, even at their worst.

Kaytee and I are supposed to meet up at the flagpole after school to walk home together. I get there before she does. I'm pretty much convinced she's already ditched me for MorganElla when she comes dashing toward me.

"Sophie!" she says breathlessly. "Did you *see* Morgan trying to kiss up to me today? Could she be any more obvious? She's only being nice to me to get to my brother . . ."

Is it possible that my kind of luck isn't always bad? That maybe, just maybe, all my lies have paid off in the best ways?

That despite all my deception, there really is no harm done?

"Look, I don't want there to be any shadiness between us," Kaytee says in that mind-reading way of hers.

I literally gag and Kaytee whacks me on the back.

"Are you okay?"

"Fine." I cough. *Just choking on all my lies,* I think.

"I sat with Morgan and Ella and Maddy at lunch today," she confesses. "Not because I wanted to. It was more like *they* sat with *me,* you know what I mean?"

I don't. MorganElla has never—will never—make such an effort for me.

"I didn't want you to find out from someone else and think I'm two-faced . . ."

At this point, I'm more like eight-faced. Sixteen-faced. Thirty-two-faced.

"So we're good?" she asks.

I mumble an okay. I appreciate Kaytee for being so honest about this, but now I feel even guiltier for being not so. Also, I don't like hearing about what's going on in the Cool House without me. I'd much rather get back into our friendship comfort zone.

"What To Do should we tackle today?"

Kaytee fills her cheeks with air just to make her sigh that much more dramatic.

"I wish I could," she says. "So much homework! Like, the teachers didn't waste any time in getting all academic on me. Didn't House Two get homework?"

Kaytee pauses at the front gate to her yard.

"You're so lucky to be in the Uncool House," she says.

I'm having trouble interpreting her expression, which is weird because Kaytee's emotions are usually spelled out in big billboard letters across her face. And before I get a chance for a second or third read, she's already gone.

WORRY DOLLS

WE'VE MADE IT THROUGH OUR FIRST WEEK AT MERCER. SHOCKINGLY, my fictional feud with Morgan over Alex is holding up. Five days in the Cool House and Kaytee is still my friend. She wants to hang out this weekend and has already bought the supplies for our next To Do. I'm optimistic that maybe nothing will change between us after all. I'm humming as I head to her house as I always do on Saturday mornings.

Never impossible . . . Always I'm possible . . .

But like never before, Kaytee isn't alone.

"Good morning, Sophie," Mrs. Ray says, greeting me at the door. "The squad is upstairs."

Squad?

"You know," she says, sensing my hesitation. "The girls."

The girls.

"Your friends?"

All my other friends.

I hear their voices before I reach the top of the stairs. Kaytee's door is shut, so I eavesdrop from the safety of the empty hallway.

"Are the boys cuter in Virginia or New Jersey?" Morgan asks.

"I haven't noticed much of a difference," Kaytee replies.

"Why aren't you on Fotobomb?" Maddy asks.

"My parents," she explains. "So overprotective."

"You can totally get around the parental controls," Maddy says. "It's easy. I could show you."

"Well," Kaytee says. "I don't have my own phone. And even if I did, that would be lying to my parents. And I don't lie."

Kaytee doesn't lie. But *I* do.

"No wonder you and goody-goody Sophie are besties!" Morgan jokes.

I should just turn around and go home but I can't move my feet.

"I'm not a goody-goody. I just don't like to lie."

I hope Kaytee will say something about me not being a goody-goody either, but she doesn't. Because that would make *her* a liar. And Kaytee doesn't lie. I'm breathing so hard and so fast now and it's not the good and calming kind. I need to move before my panting gives me away . . .

"What are you doing?"

It's Alex. Scowling. At me.

"I . . ."

RUN.

"Are you spying on my sister?"

RUN.

"I . . ."

RUUUUUUUUUN.

I grab the doorknob, fling myself into the bedroom to escape Alex the Bodyguard with Impulse Control Issues Who Totally Hates Me.

"Sophie!" Kaytee cries out. "You guys, it's Sophie!"

If outside the door is bad, inside is even worse.

Kaytee, Morgan, and Maddy are sitting one behind the other, in that order, braiding one another's hair. Ella is nowhere to be seen, which adds another layer of strangeness to the scene.

"Hey, Soph—OW!"

Kaytee tries to jump up, but Morgan is clutching two thick strands of her hair like a horseback rider on the reins.

"Sit still!" Morgan commands. "I'm not done yet."

Morgan works on an intricate pattern, making the most beautiful friendship bracelet woven from Kaytee's hair. Maddy is less successful at taming Morgan's wild waves.

"Sit down," Kaytee says, "join us!"

This is a nonsense invitation. My hands are too clumsy to braid and my hair is too short to be braided. Basic Girl 101. Fail.

Styling time is over when Morgan wraps a rubber band around the end of Kaytee's braid. Maddy does the same to Morgan's. They post pictures of one another's handiwork.

"Faboosh! Thank you!"

"No, thank *you*!"

"I love it!"

Morgan barely glances at the pic before undoing the rubber band and shaking her fiery curls free.

"Ummm . . . Kaytee?" Morgan is aggressively ignoring me. "Are you shopping with us or sticking around here for arts and crafts?"

Only then do I notice the spilled contents of a Kathy's Krafts bag on the floor. Toothpicks. Glue. Beads. The same embroidery floss we used to make our friendship bracelets. I put the clues together and come up with number 57: "Worry Dolls." These are tiny little handmade figures you tell your troubles to. Seeing Morgan and Maddy in Kaytee's room requires an entire army of worry dolls. That bag is meant for me! Not them. *Me!* This is my To Do List with Kaytee! Not theirs!

"So are you coming or *what*?" Morgan is getting huffy.

Kaytee's eyes meet mine. *Please say no,* I silently plead. *You promised.*

"Sure," Kaytee says, "but only if Sophie comes with us."

A flicker of annoyance crosses Morgan's face, but she quickly recovers. She is an actress after all. Not a great one, but good enough to trick most people most of the time. She copies the gritted-teeth, dead-eyed smile Riley Quick falls back on whenever she loses an award.

"Whatever."

Morgan and Maddy exit before I speak up.

"What are you doing?" I hiss. "The feud!"

"I'm trying to make it better so we can *all* be friends," Kaytee says. "Don't you want us to be a squad?"

No. I don't.

But it looks like someone else does.

"Promise you won't bring up Alex," I say.

She wiggles her pinkie at me but is already out the door following Morgan and Maddy before I link up to make it official.

DOWNTOWN

WE HIT FOUR CLOTHING STORES IN LESS THAN AN HOUR. ALL ARE TOO loud, too bright, and too artificially fragrant in their own toxic ways. I can't wait to leave each one.

When I told Mom I was going shopping with my "squad," she practically threw a fistful of twenties at me. I never get excited about shopping, but I want to convince Kaytee I can be someone the Cool House squad wouldn't be ashamed to be seen with in public. So in the first store I buy new glittery canvas slip-ons just like Kaytee's except mine are shot through with silver threads and hers with gold. I know my parents will approve because it's one of those philanthropic companies that donates a pair of shoes for every pair sold. Because of my purchase, there will be one less barefoot kid in an underdeveloped country.

I am totally shopped out in stores two, three, and four.

Kaytee models a cropped sweater over high-waisted jeans,

turning this way and that in front of a three-way mirror. The reflections bounce off one another, reproducing endless, infinitely stylish Kaytees.

I'm afraid none of them will ever want to go back to hanging out with me.

Just me.

"You're so much more fun than Ella!" Morgan says to Kaytee from behind the dressing room door.

"Where is Ella anyway?" I take a risk in asking.

"She said she had to help her mom with something," Morgan replies. "Whatever. No big loss. She never tries on anything anyway! I tell her all the time that she can still try stuff on even if she doesn't have any money, you know, just to see what looks cute on her."

"Everything looks cute on Ella," Maddy says. Then, as if realizing she's made the worst mistake of her life, quickly follows up with, "And you two . . . um . . . too!"

"Ugh. If it were up to my parents, I'd still wear a uniform!" Kaytee gripes.

Morgan sashays out of the dressing room in a floral romper that will not keep her warm as the seasons change. Morgan shakes her flaming mane and Kaytee steps aside. Morgan will never be as pretty as Kaytee, but she's got an undeniably gorgeous head of hair. She probably washes it in the tears of her haters. I want to whisper this observation to Kaytee but decide against it.

"Something funny?" Morgan asks.

"Nope," I reply. "Nothing is funny."

Or fun. But so far there hasn't been any mention of Alex or our fake feud or Fotobombs so I'll consider it a success.

Finally, as Kaytee would say, a *millionbilliontrillion* forevers later, Morgan decides its time for the break I was promised after the second store.

"Well, since *you're* here," Morgan says, "you might as well make yourself useful."

Then without another word, she drops her shopping bag at my right foot. After a moment's hesitation, Maddy drops hers at my left foot.

"It's almost time!" Morgan says, checking her phone. "Let's post up!"

The duo turns the corner. I bend over to pick up the shopping bags left behind on the sidewalk. I stop Kaytee when she tries to help me.

"It's okay," I say. "I don't mind."

Kaytee gives me an uncertain look before following Morgan and Maddy, empty-handed. When I reach the group, they've already arranged themselves on a bench with a clear view of the entrance to the All American Sports store.

"Perfect view!" Morgan says.

"Lacrosse players are the hottest!" Maddy says, nudging Morgan. "Don't you think?"

I'm pretty sure I'm the hottest person in Stockton Square right now. I'm so nervous, I'm one degree away from exploding into a new galaxy of tiny suns.

Maddy points at two boys in FIFA jerseys heading toward us.

"Personally, I have a thing for soccer players!"

Oh no. It's Alex and Diego. I feel set up.

Morgan stops posing for her phone long enough to punch Maddy in the arm.

"I've got dibs on Alex," Morgan says. "But Ella isn't here so Diego is fair game."

Dibs? Fair game? I'm no fan of Alex, but shouldn't he at least have a say in the matter?

"He's really here!" Morgan yelps.

"I told you he would be."

Kaytee wears a satisfied expression that's more of a smirk than a smile. I don't like it one bit. I don't like any of this. I *was* set up. But I don't have any time to contemplate why Kaytee would put me in this situation because the girls have already ambushed the boys. To my surprise, Alex looks annoyed by the disruption. Or maybe he's just annoyed that I'm crashing the cute girl party. Diego, however, is thrilled. He says something in Spanish to an older woman who I assume is his mom. I'm not fluent enough to translate, but she smiles and heads into the store without them.

"Hey, girls!" Diego calls out.

"Hey, guys!" singsong Morgan and Maddy in response.

Alex rolls his eyes. "Let's get our gear and get out," he says, pulling Diego by his arm.

"Bye, girls!" Diego says.

"Bye, guys!" singsong Morgan and Maddy.

The whole exchange takes less than five seconds, yet I already know that Morgan will be analyzing it for the rest of the day.

"Omigoddess!" Morgan squeals. "He's totally into me!"

"Omigoddess!" Maddy squeals. "He's totally into you!"

I say nothing. Again, I don't think anyone notices my silence. Or cares.

That is, until Kaytee cups her hand to my ear to whisper words of encouragement.

Because Kaytee notices.

Kaytee cares.

"Smart move, not saying anything," she says. "Morgan's gotta see you aren't interested in my brother now. So that's progress, right?"

One step forward and a millionbilliontrillion steps back.

A slow parade of old ladies in baggy polyester tracksuits pass us by on the sidewalk. One of them pumps her arms in an exaggerated way that reminds me of Ella's silly no-running-around-the-pool walk. If Ella were here, would she be thinking what I'm thinking?

"Hey, Ella," I'd say. "Remember . . . ?"

Would we have a bonding moment like we did on the mat in gym class?

I haven't even opened my mouth, and yet I've somehow reminded Morgan of my existence.

"Why are you even here again?" she asks.

Snark like this usually takes me out for good. But when Kaytee slings an arm around me, it's like the most miraculous antidote to Morgan's poisonous sting.

"Sophie's here because I want her here," Kaytee says. "She totally gets it."

I don't. Not at all. But I like that Kaytee thinks I do.

"Seriously, Sophie's so normcore," Kaytee says.

"So *what*?" Morgan asks, and I'm relieved I'm not the only one who doesn't know what that means.

"Give me your phone," Kaytee says.

Maddy hands hers over and within a few quick taps and swipes, Kaytee has found a bunch of recent paparazzi shots of Kaytee K. dressed in Eco/Echo.

"Save-the-World Normcore," Kaytee says with a smile. "So ordinary it's edgy. And environmentally friendly! It's all over the socials."

I appreciate what Kaytee is trying to do here. Since my allergic reaction to the sequins, I've resisted borrowing any more of her clothes and have gone back to my usual no-thought-required attire. There's no way MorganElla will believe I'm making any sort of fashion statement.

"Ummm . . ."

Fortunately, Morgan is already bored by this conversation and ready to move on. Unfortunately, that means she could start talking about anything. Anything at all. At any moment, Morgan could contradict my lie about fighting over Alex. So many lies could be exposed and any one of them could destroy my friendship with Kaytee . . .

Maddy thwacks me with a shopping bag.

I'm so deep into The Zone that it takes a few moments to return to reality.

"I repeat," Morgan says. "Do. You. Have. Any. Money?"

When I don't reply fast enough, Maddy thwacks me again.

"Yes!" I blurt. "I have money!"

"Congratulations!" Morgan says. "You've been promoted! You get to buy us smoothies and nachos!"

She says this as if spending *my* money to provide *them* with snacks is the ultimate privilege.

"Extra cheese!" Morgan shouts. "Or don't come back!"

Kaytee pulls me close.

"Hey, at least she's talking to you!" she says. "Progress!"

I keep hoping I'll get some insight into Morgan's personality. Like, I'll discover something about her upbringing that explains why she's so mean. It would make sense if her older sister bosses Morgan around and makes her feel bad about herself, which, in turn, makes Morgan boss us around to feel better about herself, which seems contradictory but is actually very common. Too many clients end up in my mother's office because they are caught up in the cycle of abuse.

But no such explanation comes. Morgan is mean because we let her. And because she's very, very good at it.

Do I lie because they let me?

Because I'm very, very good at it?

And getting even better?

I know I should skip Frootie Smoothie and keep walking past the Snack Shack until I'm safe at home, but I don't. I can't leave Kaytee alone with them any longer than necessary.

I'm squeezing extra melted cheese onto two take-out cartons of nachos and trying to figure out how I'm going to carry them and four large smoothies when I get nudged from behind.

"Hey, Sophie."

I've never been so happy to see Harumi. I'd hug her if my hands weren't full.

"I didn't know you were here," I say.

"We're all here," she says, gesturing with her plate.

Sofie-with-an-F, Olivia, and Harumi's mom wave at me from a table on the other side of the Snack Shack.

"We told you we were going to see the new Dragonologist movie," she says. "We asked you to come with us. Remember?"

She had. And I turned her down because I thought I'd be working on the To Do List with Kaytee.

"I'm sorry," I say. "I—"

"I guess you had better things to do," she says. "Better people to do it with." She eyes the nachos and the smoothies and suddenly puts two and two together. "I guess *someone*'s gotta buy Morgan's snacks. No offense! I mean, maybe that's fun for *you*."

I have nothing convincingly positive to say in response.

"So that new girl Kaytee is pretty tight with them, huh?" she asks.

"She's my friend, remember? Not Morgan's."

"Oh," she says. "Well, I've seen her around school with Morgan and Ella so . . ."

Of course she thinks Kaytee is now Morgan's friend, not mine anymore. It's obvious that Kaytee should be friends with someone like Morgan instead of someone like me.

"But I guess that sort of explains why you're with them now," she says. "Sofie, Olivia, and I couldn't figure it out."

Right. Because there'd have to be a very good reason why Morgan would ever be seen anywhere near an ICKFACE RANDO WEIRDO.

"Well, you better hurry," Harumi warns. "Morgan likes her smoothies cold and her nachos nice and hot."

When I get back to the bench in front of All American Sports, Morgan takes one look at my delivery and grimaces.

"You took too long. The smoothie is too warm and those nachos are too cold."

I look to Kaytee for another resuscitating smile, but she just nods in agreement.

"Do you want me to *die* of food poisoning?" Morgan asks. "Consider yourself demoted."

As I toss the untouched drinks and nachos into the trash, I have to ask myself: What's worse than losing the "privilege" of purchasing Morgan's snacks? I have a sinking feeling it won't take very long to find out.

WHAT'S WORSE?

ON THE WALK TO SCHOOL THIS MORNING, IT SEEMS LIKE EVERYTHING
will be better.

At first.

Until it gets worse.

Way worse.

"Are you okay, Sophie?" Kaytee asks. "I was kind of worried about you on Saturday."

"What do you mean?"

"Well, you got really quiet," she says, "even for you."

After my demotion, the talk turned to boys I don't think are cute, influencers I don't follow, music I don't listen to, makeup I don't wear, clothes I don't own, memes I don't know. Basic Girl 101. So I didn't have much to contribute for the rest of the afternoon. Not that I could've mustered the courage to do so, even if I did. Kaytee talked enough for the both of us.

"All that shopping wore me out," I say.

I'm waiting for her to compliment me on my only purchase that day.

"Okay," she says. "Good."

I step around bird poop on the sidewalk. I don't want to get my new shoes dirty.

"So there's something I want to talk to you about," she says.

We walk ten paces before she speaks again. I'm suddenly aware of how flat-footed my steps are in these shoes. They have very little arch support. And the back seam rubs against my Achilles tendon.

"I won't be able to walk home from school with you today," she says. "And most days from now on."

I stumble on a rock.

"Why not?" I ask, righting myself.

"I'm trying out for a travel soccer team."

She takes three jogging steps and skillfully kicks the rock that tripped me. It whizzes down the sidewalk into an invisible goal. Score.

"It's too late for me to play for Mercer's school team, so the travel team is the next best thing."

"Travel team? But soccer is Alex's thing! You don't even like soccer!"

I've seen Alex and Kaytee messing around with a soccer ball, but I always assumed it was his idea of fun, not hers.

"I *do* like soccer. I played on teams back in Virginia and I'm really good. Maybe even better than Alex."

We're stopped at the crosswalk right in front of the school, waiting for the traffic safety officer to wave us through.

"Morgan is trying out too," she says casually.

My silver shoes turn to stone.

Morgan? Trying out for a *sport*? No way. Either Morgan thinks she's trying out for *Soccer: The Musical!* or Kaytee is mixing up her Morgans. *Someone* is wrong here.

"Morgan says the most popular eighth graders play travel soccer."

Now that's an explanation that *sort of* makes sense. But there's got to be a less sweaty path to popularity.

"Morgan played for another league all summer," Kaytee continues. "But you know that."

I didn't know that. And why should I? Morgan and I have never been—will never be—friends.

The officer is giving us the walk signal, but I can't move.

"I don't think Morgan even *likes* playing soccer," Kaytee says. "It's just, like, another thing to add to her résumé to make herself look better than everyone else. It's a little annoying, honestly."

I'm surprised—and encouraged—by the irritated shift in Kaytee's tone.

"Well, if she's so annoying," I say, "why try out to be on the same soccer team?"

Kaytee busts out laughing.

"I'm not trying out for soccer because of *Morgan*," she says. "Morgan's trying out for soccer because of *me*."

Kaytee makes this announcement with a level of popular-girl

confidence that only comes with experience. I was so afraid of MorganElla influencing Kaytee that I hadn't even considered the opposite could happen. But if anyone's capable of taming the girl-beast, it's Kaytee. How dangerously close will she have to get to MorganElla before such a transformation is possible? And what's to stop Kaytee from liking this new-and-improved MorganElla more than she likes me?

"Love the new shoes by the way," Kaytee says when we reach the stairwell where we go our separate ways every day.

Kaytee notices.

Kaytee cares.

Kaytee is still my friend.

And that's enough to help me make it through an entire day without needing to breathe, count, release, and repeat.

DO SOMETHING

KAYTEE MADE THE SOCCER TEAM. MORGAN DID TOO. WHICH ISN'T surprising because Morgan always gets what she wants. And yet totally surprising because I still can't get over the concept of Morgan playing soccer. So I haven't seen much of Kaytee all week, just in the mornings on walks to school that are getting shorter and shorter and shorter even though logically I know the distance hasn't changed.

The walks home alone are getting longer and longer and longer.

This is also illogical. The distance measures the same both ways.

But it's reassuring to see the extra spot at our dinner table tonight. All four sides of the square are occupied. It's been three weeks since Kaytee started at Mercer and her presence here on a Friday night makes good on her promise. She's sleeping over at *my* house, which proves that we are still friends despite whatever is happening in the Cool House, on the soccer field, or wherever else.

Without me.

"Thank you so much for rescuing me!" Kaytee says. "I *so* didn't want to go to the Wilson thingie."

Mr. and Mrs. Ray are attending Alex's parent/teacher night. Kaytee begged to be left behind and my mom in particular was more than happy to have her over. I thought this hospitality was strangely social of her until I discovered her ulterior motives.

"It's our pleasure!" my mom says, setting down the tray of hot pizza. "Maybe now I can find out what's happening in seventh grade, because I can't get any details from this one at all!"

It takes a moment for me to realize that the "this one" she's referring to is me. I've been a seventh grader for two months. And I have no idea what's "happening," at least not in the ways my mom is interested in hearing about. She gets clients to open up to her all day. I wonder if my silence frustrates her. Or makes her question her social-working skills.

Kaytee waits until Mom goes to the kitchen to get a pizza cutter before leaning into the tray and giving it a curious sniff.

"Vegan cheese made from cashews, and tofu pepperoni," I explain. "It tastes just like the real thing."

"Ummm. How would you know how the real thing tastes?"

The *ummm* lands with a thud in my heart.

Kaytee is a tone-deaf singer but in just three weeks she has nailed Morgan's G3 below middle C.

Ummm . . .

If Kaytee hadn't ummmed at me, I might have told her how I used to sneak slices whenever I slept over at Ella's house. I'd brush and floss and mouthwash and chew gum so my parents wouldn't detect the forbidden meat on my breath. I'm realizing right now that I miss real pizza with real pepperoni way more than I miss Ella. Even House Two losers know she's the prettiest girl in the whole seventh grade. I think Kaytee is prettier because she's nicer, but I'm terrified of eyelash curlers so I'm not the best judge of middle school beauty.

"You left Villa Academy to attend Mercer Middle," Dad says, raising his glass of iced green tea in triumph. "What a victory for the public school system!"

"Now tell us, Kaytee," Mom says, heaping the last of the organic farm's summer lettuce into our salad bowls. "What's your impression of Mercer Middle so far?"

"I love it!"

Kaytee pinches a weedy-looking green from her bowl and gives it a good look before putting it back.

"Please tell us all about it," my mother says.

And for the rest of the meal, Kaytee entertains my parents with stories from her first three weeks of seventh grade.

She tells us that she wakes up every morning so psyched to get dressed because when she chooses an outfit, she's telling the world what kind of girl she wants to be that day. Sometimes she's silly and sparkly, sometimes she's stretchy and sporty, sometimes she's serious and studious. She tells us she wants to burn her Villa

Academy uniform and will never, ever, ever let anyone tell her what she can and can't wear ever again.

(I think she's being unreasonable. But that's because I am unfashionable. To me, wearing a school uniform is one of the most appealing aspects of private school.)

She tells us how she couldn't open up her locker and a boy whose locker is right next to hers tried to help her by banging it open with his fist and of course it didn't work. Then she realized she'd mixed up all the numbers so now she sings the digits to herself to the tune of the Kaytee K. song "Open Up," which the boy whose locker is right next to hers thinks is funny but her homeroom/social studies teacher says is distracting.

(I opened up my locker on the first try. I have not talked to any boys unless instructed to do so by a teacher for academic purposes. I do my best to blend in. I never sing. I'll never sing again.)

She tells us how she loves switching classes because if she doesn't like a certain teacher she's not tortured for every single minute of every day like at Villa Academy, but for only fifty minutes a day, which is totally survivable because then the bell rings and you move on to another teacher you like waaaay better, which is how she feels about her homeroom/social studies ("BOOOOO!") and language arts ("YAAAAY!") teachers.

(Dad always says I don't have to like my teachers, I just have to learn from them. I've gotten all As so far, even in Señora Mar-TEEN's class, where I'm doing mucho extra credit to make up for my lackluster class participation grade.)

She tells us how lunch is her favorite period because it's all

217

about socializing and she's relieved Morgan and Ella and Maddy invited her to sit with them on the first day because otherwise she would've maybe sat by herself but it's a bummer that I'm not there to gossip and giggle along with them.

"Wait," I interrupt. "I thought *they* sat with *you*."

"Right!" Kaytee says. "Whatever. Same difference, right?"

(Wrong. It makes all the difference in the world.)

I watch Dad eat three slices with all the crusts, and salad.

Mom eats two slices minus the crusts, and salad.

I eat one slice, Mom's crusts, and salad.

Kaytee talks and talks and talks but eats nothing. Is this how she spends her favorite part of her day, every day? Because lunch is more about socializing than eating? I see Kaytee when House Two enters the cafeteria and House One exits. The first two weeks, Kaytee smiled, waved, and said hi to me. This week, she did the same on Monday, Tuesday, Wednesday, and Thursday. But Friday—today—she was too caught up in conversation with MorganElla and Maddy to notice me.

Am I getting too good at blending in?

Inhale.

Expand the belly.

Count to three.

Exhale.

Squeeze the belly.

Count to three.

"And there are so many clubs! I don't know how I'm going to choose . . ."

"Wait!"

My parents recoil at my raised voice.

"Sophie," Mom says. "It's rude to keep interrupting."

"I thought we decided to join the DoSomething club together," I say, ignoring my mother. "On the days you don't have soccer practice."

My social studies teacher, Mr. Schwartzman, interrupted our lesson on the impact of China's geographic isolation on its culture to announce that he got approval to start a chapter of the DoSomething club at Mercer. It's an organization dedicated to community service projects, and Harumi and Sofie-with-an-F want to sign up because they think Mr. Schwartzman is cute with his glasses and his floppy hair, but EWW he's a *teacher*. I'm joining so Mom will stop hassling me about extracurriculars every Tuesday and Thursday afternoon. This seemed like the best option because philanthrophy thrills my parents almost as much as it thrills Mr. Schwartzman. And after seeing her commitment to completing my To Do List, I thought it would thrill Kaytee too.

Up to this very moment, I thought she agreed with me.

She takes a sip of water. "The DoSomething club. Right. I forgot. I'm sorry."

"The DoSomething club," Mom says, rising from the table. "You haven't said anything about it to me, Sophie. Are you sure you mentioned it to Kaytee?"

"It's a symptom of affluenza," Dad mutters, following Mom into the kitchen. "The paralyzing paradox of too many choices."

I wait until my parents are loading the dishwasher before confronting her.

"You *forgot* about DoSomething club? We were just talking about it yesterday!"

"I didn't forget, I just didn't remember right away," Kaytee says. "I'm sorry! My locker combination takes up too much of my brainspace."

She crosses her eyes and sticks out her tongue to make me laugh. But now I'm too concerned to think it's very funny. The brain needs fuel to function.

"Aren't you going to eat anything?"

Kaytee picks up the now cold slice of pizza and sniffs yet again. She squints. She nibbles the tiniest piece off the tip.

"BLEEEEEEECH."

She spits it out into a napkin. She gargles with a mouthful of water. She scrubs her tongue with a piece of lettuce from her salad. I'm expecting my dad to shoot my mom a disapproving look. Kaytee's grossed-out facial contortions would be hilarious if I weren't worried that they were hiding a not-so-funny secret. Is this what happens when you're already shy about your body because you were bullied at your old school and are suddenly surrounded by girls who obsess over their appearances at your new school . . . ?

"I take it you're not a fan of vegan pizza," Mom says with a laugh as she clears Kaytee's plate. "Not everyone is."

I'm shocked that my mother of all people can't see what's really going on here. Maybe my amateur diagnosis isn't as accurate as

I assumed? Or maybe Kaytee is just really, really good at hiding the truth? Now I'm concerned *and* confused. I don't know for sure what Kiera did to Kaytee back in Virginia. And I haven't witnessed with my own eyes what goes on with MorganElla during House One's lunch period every day.

But I can see what's happening right now in front of me.

BEST FRIENDS

ALONE TOGETHER IN MY BEDROOM. I PRETEND TO BE A GOOD hostess.

"Chips?"

I'm offering a bag of sprouted bean crisps I snagged from the pantry and snuck upstairs. My parents don't allow food outside the kitchen. But I think they would agree that this rule breaking is for a good cause.

Kaytee politely declines, as I was afraid she would. I try harder.

"They taste just like . . ."

"Just like regular potato chips," she says. "I know. But no thanks."

"Okay," I say, "then let's get all comfy in our PJs before we get started on number forty-three."

It feels like a millionbilliontrillion forevers since I opened *The Book of Awesome for Awesome Girls* when in reality it's only been three days. Tonight we're supposed to learn how to play an Arabic marble game. But there's something far more important that needs to happen first.

"Okaaay," Kaytee says.

I go straight to my dresser drawer and pull out my favorite set of pajamas. I kick off my khakis and step into fleece bottoms. I whip off my sweater and pull a waffle-knit tee over my head.

"Ready for Mancala?"

As I'd expected, Kaytee is hesitant to undress. Her back is to me as she fiddles with her opened overnight bag.

"Do you mind if I use your bathroom?"

Her pajamas are slung over the crook of her arm.

"I do mind."

Kaytee flinches. "What do you mean?"

This confrontation will be awkward, but totally worth it if Kaytee realizes it's for her own good.

"I know your secret," I say. "I know about Kiera."

Kaytee couldn't look more stunned.

"Y-y-you d-do?" she stammers.

"She made you embarrassed to be a late bloomer," I say. "She made you feel like everyone is growing up and leaving you behind."

"She . . . ?" Kaytee asks, clearly in shock.

It's the closest I've come to telling her the truth about MorganElla. Can I go all the way?

"I don't know what she did to you, and you don't have to tell me if you don't want to," I insist. "But I know what it feels like to be excluded. I never thought I'd get my first period. And then I did!" I conveniently leave out the part that I've only gotten it once so it's still pretty new to me. "And you will too!"

Kaytee furrows her brow.

"I've read all about bad body image in my mom's books," I say. "And I'm afraid that after whatever happened between you and Kiera, spending time with Morgan and Ella and Maddy is making you feel insecure all over again."

Kaytee frowns.

"But I just want to tell you before anything else that you have an awesome body! Like, think of all the things you can do with your body. Like making the travel soccer team! Or walking on your hands. I wish I had the strength to walk on my hands. Do you remember that you were walking on your hands when we first met?" Kaytee shakes her head in a dazed sort of way. "You were out on the lawn walking on your hands like it is no big whoop."

Kaytee's face flattens out. The blank expression is weirdly unreadable, so I keep going.

"I failed the physical fitness test!"

Kaytee closes her eyes. Tears slip through her lashes and down her cheeks. My message is getting through to her!

"So let's focus on good nutrition and maybe we can even get my mom to recommend a therapist who specializes in these issues," I say. "Let's help you get over whatever hang-ups you've got about your body and food, because I can name plenty of girls who wish they were more like you!"

Starting with me.

A battle breaks out over Kaytee's face. The upper half is still crying, but the lower half is now laughing uncontrollably like *hahasniffsniffblubberblubber*.

It's the most intense mix of emotions I've ever witnessed.

"You're so wrong," Kaytee says, voice shaking. "You have no idea how wrong you are."

She takes a huge breath, holds it, and lets it go.

She takes another huge breath, holds it, and lets it go.

After the third round, I catch on to what she's doing.

She's inhaling.

Expanding the belly.

Counting to three.

Exhaling.

Squeezing the belly.

Counting to three.

She learned the technique from watching me.

"We're best friends, right?" Kaytee asks.

The question thrills me to the core.

"Right!"

We're best friends.

Does everyone see us that way? If you polled all seventh grade students in House One and House Two, if you asked, "Who is Kaytee Ray's best friend?" would the unanimous answer be "Sophie Dailey"?

"You know me better than anyone in New Jersey, but I've been keeping something from you," she says. "And it's not about being a late bloomer. Not really."

It hurts me to hear that she's still in denial.

"Kaytee, it's okay," I assure her. "I won't judge you for . . ."

She cuts me off.

"I turn down your snacks because brussels sprout chips are gross."

"Sprouted bean chips," I correct.

"Whatever! Either way, they're gross, but not as gross as the vegan pizza, which—no offense to your mom—was the grossest thing ever, which is why I spit it out."

She crosses the space between us and sits beside me.

"If I tell you the truth, you have to promise you won't say a word to anyone."

I nod.

"I mean it," Kaytee says. "You have to promise you won't tell anyone. Ever. Not Morgan. Not Ella. Not Maddy or anyone else at school. Our friendship depends on it."

I promise without hesitation. All at once Kaytee crushes me in a hug, literally taking my breath away.

"I don't deserve you as a friend!" she cries.

"Of course you d—"

Kaytee releases me, cuts me off.

"No! I don't! And when you find out why, you'll agree with me."

"Kaytee . . ."

"My name isn't Kaytee!"

Her . . . name . . . isn't . . .

Kaytee?

She takes in my confused expression and repeats the words, quieter this time. "My name isn't Kaytee."

Her name isn't Kaytee.

As startling as this confession *should* be, it doesn't come as a total shock.

Her name isn't Kaytee.

I mean, it explains why I couldn't find *anything* about Kaytee Ray from Virginia in my extremely thorough online sleuthing. Her parents did work in Washington, DC, for many years. Is she from a family of spies? Are they in the witness protection program? What better place to hide than Mercer, New Jersey . . . ?

Her real name isn't Kaytee.

Whatever her explanation, it won't change how I feel about our friendship . . .

Until it does.

"*I'm* Kiera," she says. "*I'm* the bully."

WHAT HAPPENS NEXT

BRAINCHATTERTUMMYRUMBLEHEARTPAN
GBRAINCHATTERTUMMYRUMBLEHEARTPANGB
RAINCHATTERTUMMYRUMBLEHEARTPANGBRAIN
CHATTERTUMMYRUMBLEHEARTPANGBRAIN
CHATTERTUMMYRUMBLEHEARTPANGBRAINCH
ATTERTUMMYRUMBLEHEARTPANGBRAIN
CHATTERTUMMYRUMBLEHEARTPANGBRAIN
CHATTERTUMMYRUMBLEHEARTPANGBRAINCH
ATTERTUMMYRUMBLEHEARTPANGBRAINC
HATTERTUMMYRUMBLEHEARTPANGBRAIN
CHATTERTUMMYRUMBLEHEARTPANGBRAINC
HATTERTUMMYRUMBLEHEARTPANGBRAIN
CHATTERTUMMYRUMBLEHEARTPANG
BRAINCHATTERTUMMYRUMBLEHEARTPANG
BRAINCHATTERTUMMYRUMBLEHEARTPANG

BRAINCHATTERTUMMYRUMBLEHEARTPANG
BRAINCHATTERTUMMYRUMBLEHEART
PANGBRAINCHATTERTUMMYRUMBLEHEART
PANGBRAINCHATTERTUMMYRUMBLE
HEARTPANGBRAINCHATTERTUMMYRUMBLE
HEARTPANGBRAINCHATTERTUMMYRUMBLE
HEARTPANGBRAINCHATTERTUMMYRU

I can't hear anything over the sound of my own anxiety. And I honestly don't know how long I've been sitting here—watching Kaytee's lips move but hearing nothing—before her words start breaking through the chaos in my mind.

"So I'm not shy about my body, I'm just paranoid that some girl will do to me what I did to her," she's saying. "Like, karma."

I'm out of The Zone now, back to reality, fully conscious of everything that's happening between us. But wishing I weren't.

"I swore I wouldn't tell anyone because I wanted a fresh start. But then I met you, and, I don't know why, but my heart told me you could be trusted. That if we were really best friends, I should tell you. And I came close at the beach house, but I was too scared . . ."

"Too scared to tell me what? That you're pretending to be my friend?"

Kaytee hugs her knees and rocks back and forth.

"I'm not pretending," she says softly. "You're my best friend in New Jersey or anywhere else."

Her real name isn't Kaytee. I know nothing about . . . Kiera Ray.

"You lied to me," I say, "about everything."

I suddenly feel so stupid for ever worrying about my own deceit. Even my biggest whoppers are nothing—NOTHING—compared with this!

"I never *lied*," she says firmly. "I just didn't give you the fullest truth . . ."

I can't believe she's using Kaytee K. to defend the indefensible! She's actually twisting lyrics about building trust through honesty to excuse her shady behavior! That's the exact opposite of what the song is about! What's worst of all? She thinks I'm gullible enough to fall for her bogus best friendship routine all over again. And why shouldn't she? She's gotten away with faking sincerity for this long; why stop now?

All my anxiety disappears and is replaced with an emotion I'm not used to feeling:

Anger.

"I can't even look at you right now," I say. "You need to leave."

"Soph—"

I turn my back on her, on our friendship. I don't make another move until I know Kaytee—Kiera Tessa Ray—is gone.

From my room.

From my life.

For good?

PART FOUR

AWKWARD CONVERSATION CUPCAKES

I STAYED UP TOO LATE TRYING TO LEARN AS MUCH AS I POSSIBLY could about Kiera Tessa Ray on the Internet. Despite my many attempts to craft the perfect combination of admittedly limited search terms (*Kiera Tessa Ray Virginia*), it isn't much. She was a soccer star. She made the elementary school honor roll. She and Alex participated in a Twin Parade at the Virginia State Fair.

There's nothing about getting expelled.

Or being a bully.

But that makes sense. She's only a kid, so it's illegal to make her name public without her parents' permission. It's not like the Rays would proudly blast their daughter's bad behavior across all the socials. And Mrs. Ray worked in PR, so she would know better than anyone how to scrub the Internet of any negative news that managed to sneak through. All the juiciest gossip is intentionally unsearchable. Apps like Fotobomb are designed to do damage—BOOM!—then disappear. And yet, I keep at it. Hoping to find any information at all that can make sense of what I learned about this person I thought was my best friend.

I'm well into my twelfth hour of futile sleuthing when the doorbell rings.

DING-DONG!

The weird thing is, I'm not startled by the sudden break in the silence. Maybe I'm too exhausted to react. Maybe I've been expecting it to happen all morning. Another dreaded inevitable.

DING-DONG!

If I peek out my bedroom window from behind my curtains, I can see without being seen. As I suspected, it's Kiera Tessa Ray on our doorstep. She's holding a dome-shaped Tupperware container by the handle.

She looks the same as always.

She looks like Kaytee.

I can't help but still think of her as Kaytee.

She rings the doorbell again.

DING-DONG!

No one answers. She rings the doorbell two more times. Still no one answers. She rings the doorbell to the beat of "Never Impossible."

Ne-ver im-poss-i-ble

Al-ways I'm poss-i-ble.

Dad finally answers the bell. I can't see him, but I imagine he looks all stressed out like he does when he gets interrupted. When he opens the door to Kaytee on the porch, his face will rearrange itself into something softer.

"Special delivery!" Kaytee cheerfully holds up the container. "Awkward Conversation Cupcakes!"

I imagine Dad's mouth turning up at the corners.

"Awkward Conversation Cupcakes," he repeats. "That's funny."

As far as my parents know, Kaytee went home early last night because she wasn't feeling well, a lie that conveniently coincided with her stomach-turning reaction to the vegan pizza served at dinner.

"I'm so sorry, Kaytee," Dad says now. "Sophie is a little under the weather herself today."

I told Dad I was feeling "crampy." That was all he needed to hear.

"Can you give this to her?"

I see his hand reach out to take an envelope.

"A *letter*?" His voice is pitched high with genuine surprise. "Is this one of the To Dos from that book?"

I can see why my dad would think this. *Communicate the old-fashioned way. Write a letter!* sounds just like an Awesome Girls task to cross off our list.

Kaytee looks up at my window. I duck behind my curtains, but I don't think I'm fast enough.

"Nope," Kaytee says, "I came up with this all on my own."

THE LETTER

Dear Sophie,

I really, really hope you read this.

I never lied to you. I was who I was. I am who I am. I just didn't tell you the full truth. It's like the Kaytee K. song: "Give me the FULLEST truth . . ."

I would. Right now. I have so much to say if you were willing to listen. It's so weird that you're right next door but a million-billiontrillion miles away.

Kaytee K.'s autobiography is my favorite book even though I know I'm supposed to say *To Kill a Mockingbird* or something impressive like that. But I don't care, no book speaks to me like *My Krazy Life So Far*. In it Kaytee K. encourages all her Kayters to create a Life Events Timeline because "to understand where we're headed, we need to examine where we've been." She's had a lot of ups and downs in her twenty-five years. I've only been around halfish as long as Kaytee K. and most of the major stuff only happened in, like, the last three years or so, but my timeline is already pretty eventful!

When I was born, I already had a best friend. Alex is six minutes older than I am and I've been trying to catch up with him ever since.

When we were toddlers, Alex and I did everything together. I don't have any solid memories from those years, only a sense of always having my brother right beside me. We didn't have a secret language but we did call each other by private twin names: Lexi for him. KT for me.

When we were three years old, Alex and I watched way too many videos while our parents were working. I got obsessed with the pink-haired mermaid who sang "Oh Oh Ocean." She was the most gorgeous creature I'd ever seen on or off a screen. And "Kaytee" sounded just like "KT"! Alex developed a fascination with the dimpled Apple Pie cutie with the ukulele. Kayter vs. Ribot was the first major rift in our twin relationship. Maybe we toddlers battled over stuffed animals or whatever before that, but I don't remember.

Anyway.

When I was between four and eight years old, I was a happy kid. Playdates, birthday parties, sleepovers, plenty of partners for group projects. Not popular exactly, but never without a good friend or two, like Allie and Gracie, the girls in the Halloween photo I didn't want to talk about.

When I was nine years old, the bullying began.

I was the target, not the tormentor.

I've always been smaller than kids my age. And being the youngest in the grade makes it even worse. I was the tiniest girl in my class, but I was also the most athletic. I thank all the years of competing with Alex for that! Boys liked me because I played as hard as they did, whether it was kickball in gym class or zombie tag on the playground. I often got picked for teams before the less athletic boys, which was very embarrassing for them but thrilling for me. I was proud to get attention for my toughness.

But it made the other girls jealous.

A certain girl—I'll call her Bee—started spreading vicious rumors about me kissing every boy in the grade. Gross! Bee somehow made it make sense to roast me for being both too mature and immature at the same time. So she also got all the girls to throw vitamins and tell me to "grow up." The words stung, sure, but what hurt most was how quickly Allie and Gracie joined in. I realize now it was probably for their own protection, but I didn't see it that way at the time. And Bee was so smart to bully me only when Alex or an adult couldn't catch her in the act. Bee really was an evil genius . . . but that doesn't mean she deserves what I did to her.

I know I should've talked to my parents or a teacher, but I was afraid that telling an adult would only make it worse. I felt helpless and hopeless. So to survive this daily torture, I did what I always did when I wanted to get better at soccer or anything else: I studied the pros. I watched and learned from Bee's viciousness. Over time I got better at being a bully than she ever was.

When I was ten years old, I started sixth grade. I was determined to take Bee down. And I did. Literally.

I discovered a terrible talent I never knew I had. I had an eye for capturing Bee's most humiliating moments on camera. I noticed when a tiny booger dangled from her nose, or when her maxi pad bulged like a diaper or . . . you get the idea. Maybe others noticed too, only I had the nerve to snap and post the pics on Fotobomb. I'm too embarrassed to tell you ALL the truly heinous things I did to make Bee as miserable as she made me. But if I'm telling you the Fullest Truth, I have to tell you the worst of what I did.

I quietly followed her into the girls' bathroom. And . . . I'll spare you the grossest details, but she saw me waiting for her with my phone out when she exited the stall. She knew I'd made an audio of all the normal human body noises that happen when humans go to the bathroom. And she decided she'd rather escape out a window than face another humiliation on the socials.

Don't worry! The bathroom was on the first floor! Bee got away with barely a scratch. But her mom was a lawyer and threatened to sue my family on grounds of "emotional violence" and the school for "gross negligence" if I wasn't expelled. Alex and my parents all became outcasts. So I'm responsible for not only bringing shame upon myself—but my family. And there was nothing I could do—community service, therapy, and countless apologies— to make up for the damage I had already done.

By the way, the only person brave enough to stand up to my monstrous behavior during my sixth grade reign of terror was

Alex. He told me over and over again that hate is no way to fight hate. And what did he get for his goodness? Punched in the face by Bee's big brother. So when my dad was offered a transfer to New Jersey, we all were grateful for the opportunity to start over again.

When I was eleven and five-sixths years old, we moved to New Jersey. I wasn't sad about leaving. I didn't have anyone in Virginia to say goodbye to because nobody's parents wanted their daughters hanging around me anymore, which I totally deserved. I was thrilled to have a fresh start, to be the kinder version of myself I used to be. When I asked my parents to call me Kaytee, I told them it was a tribute to my favorite singer. They actually supported my decision, which was honestly a shock because my parents do not appreciate Kaytee K.'s many musical and charitable contributions to the world. I didn't share the real reason I wanted to be called Kaytee. I was inspired by the private nickname from my nicest, most innocent days. I was surprised when Alex still gave me a hard time about it though, and not because he's a Ribot through and through. He wasn't convinced a change in name meant a change of heart.

I don't blame Alex for not believing in me. I have a hard time believing in myself.

So I arrived in New Jersey as Kaytee Ray. It wasn't a perfect reset, but close. The meaner me would've thrived at Villa Academy—but I hated that girl. I liked who I was when I was with you. Your openness and honesty brought me back to my best self, before I got so good at being bad. I kept the picture of Allie and Gracie to remind me of what I'd lost. If I'd had a true friend like you in Virginia, I wouldn't have turned into a monster. The more we worked on *The Book of Awesome for Awesome Girls* together, the more I wanted to tell you about my past. We had gotten so close so quickly and it felt strange for you not to know. You were my best friend, after all.

A month after I turned twelve, I found out I was wrong.

But I hope I'm wrong about that too. I want us to be friends again.

Miss you already,
Kaytee

P.S. This is the longest letter I've written in my whole Krazy life!

Kaytee's letter gives me a lot to think about.

Too much to think about.

Breathe in.

Breathe out.

Breathe in.

Breathe out.

Breathe.

Just breathe, Sophie.

Repeat. Repeat. Repeat.

OTHER GIRLS

THE NEXT DAY I KEEP HEARING PARTS OF THE LETTER IN KAYTEE'S voice.

I felt helpless and hopeless.
I discovered a terrible talent I never knew I had.
You were my best friend, after all.

The soothing ocean waves setting on my white noise machine can't drown out the sound of Kaytee's words inside my head. It's a one-sided conversation I can't shut up, loud and persistent enough to make it impossible to think about anything else. If what she says in The Letter is true, there might be hope for us after all. Maybe a mean girl can be rehabilitated. Mom says too many of her clients clean up their acts but go back to being messy when no one gives them a second chance. There's still a lot

I don't understand about Kaytee's choices—before and after she moved here—but I never will if I don't make an effort to hear her out.

I check out the window. The Rays' yard is clear, so this might be my best chance to get answers from Kaytee without a confrontation with her twin. I cautiously head out the front door and I'm halfway to my destination when Diego chases Alex across his front lawn.

Alex.

The only person brave enough to stand up to my monstrous behavior during my sixth grade reign of terror.

Alex in The Letter sounds like a kind person, but he's been nothing but rude to me. Should I turn right around and spend the rest of Sunday hiding in my bedroom? Or do I bravely go forward to make up with my best friend? I'm still debating my options when Alex calls out.

"Yo, Sophie!"

It's the first time he's ever called me by name. And yet it still feels like a mistake.

"Me?"

"You see another Sophie?"

Sofie-with-an-F isn't around. I'm not mishearing the *ph* this time. I guess I have no choice but to slowly make my way to the other side of our shared fence.

"Yo, Diego," Alex says. "Go inside and get us something to eat."

He looks at Alex, then at me, then back to Alex again.

"I thought you skipped meals to feed on your enemies' pain."

"Ha-ha," Alex deadpans.

He told me over and over again that hate is no way to fight hate.

"Food knows the only safe place from your furious fists," Diego jokes, "is inside your own body."

"Ha."

"You don't eat. You hold food hostage."

"Okay, Diego," Alex says, punching him in the shoulder. "That's enough."

Diego jogs inside.

"I told him I got kicked out of my old school for getting in a fistfight," Alex says. "Now I've got a reputation as a tough guy."

And what did he get for his goodness? Punched in the face.

"Oh," I say.

"So," he says.

"So," I say.

He looks behind him to make sure Diego is in the house, then motions for me to come closer. Close enough to see that he's got just the faintest hint of blond hair growing on his upper lip.

"You know what Kaytee did," he says.

"Yes," I say. "I know what she did. And I know her name isn't Kaytee. It's Kiera."

Alex doesn't flinch.

"She prefers Kaytee now," he says. "So . . ."

But the conversation ends there as Diego charges back out with a doughnut in each hand.

"America runs on Dunkin'," Diego says, "but you run on the blood of your enemies!"

Alex grabs the chocolate doughnut, kicks up the soccer ball, and starts bouncing it on his knee.

"Kaytee's not here," Alex says casually as if the last five seconds haven't happened. "She's at that girl's house."

"What girl's house?"

"The annoying one with the clowny hair," he says. "They're making a video or something."

Any pleasure I might have gotten from hearing Morgan described as "the annoying one with the clowny hair" is obliterated by the news that Kaytee is with her right now, probably plotting new and creative ways to make my life miserable.

"But Kaytee doesn't even like Morgan!"

"You sure about that?"

Alex raises his eyebrows. They're much bushier than his twin's. I realize now that Kaytee must pluck them into their expressive arches. I can't imagine ever caring enough about my brows to hold a tweezer anywhere near my eyes.

"The other girls are there too."

"What girls?" I ask, even though the answer is obvious. I guess I need to hear it for myself.

"You know the ones," Alex says, taking a huge bite out of the doughnut. "Your friends. The squad."

Diego is suddenly very interested in this conversation.

"The ones from downtown?"

Alex nods. Diego fans himself with a doughnut.

"Your friends are hotties," he says. "En fuego."

"They are not my friends," I say emphatically.

"Yeah, well." Alex polishes off the doughnut, then lets the ball drop. "I guess they're all Kaytee's friends now."

MYSTERY KAYTEE

I HAVE TO SEE IT FOR MYSELF. JUST TO CONFIRM MY WORST FEARS.

I mean, Alex has never been a big fan of mine. His sister isn't home, but that doesn't mean what he's telling me about making a video at Morgan's house is true . . . does it? I log on and see right away that Morgan & Ella just uploaded a new video. But only Morgan is featured in the screen grab. So I'm feeling the tiniest bit hopeful that Alex was mistaken—at best—or messing with me—at worst.

"Today I'm helping my friend Mystery Kaytee," Morgan announces to her followers.

The minuscule spark of optimism is snuffed out for good. I know I should slam the laptop shut before it gets even worse, but I can't stop myself from watching what happens next.

"Mystery Kaytee needs to finish a silly To Do List," Morgan continues. "So she can move on with her life."

Her silly To Do List? Move on with *her* life?

"She has to write and perform a song," Morgan explains.

Write and perform a song. Number 45. The Impossible To Do. The one I couldn't To Do because MorganElla stole my voice.

"Mystery Kaytee wrote the song," Morgan says. "But she can't sing and her parents are totally overprotective and won't give her permission to appear on camera anyway even if she could. Which is why she's Mystery Kaytee."

Now Mr. and Mrs. Rays' no-social-media policy makes perfect sense. What if Bee or anyone else from Virginia caught a glimpse of Kaytee Ray on YouTube? Kiera Tessa Ray's new "good girl" identity would be exposed as a sham.

"It's a total rip-off of 'A Princess Story,' so don't sue us, Kaytee K.!" Morgan jokes. "Mystery Kaytee stole it, not me!"

I've heard the melody many, many times. But when Morgan sings, the lyrics are different. This version is about a Monster Princess born without a voice who dances to express herself. But Princess doesn't feel sorry for herself because she has so many words in her head and her heart. If she can't tell the world how she feels, she'll show it. She'll dance with grace and strength. But no one sees her beautiful body language. They see the ugliest Monster ever, with a spiky skull, bloody eyes, oozing sores, and razor fangs. When Princess sees her reflection, she sees shiny, honey hair and bright eyes and pink cheeks and rose petal lips. She sees someone as beautiful as her movements but also bold and fearless too.

The chorus goes like this:

Please see me as I really am,
You're not looking hard enough.
I'm a Princess Warrior, that's who I am,
Not made of monster stuff.

I imagine Kaytee holding the camera. Unseen.

But smiling, smiling, smiling.

"You are totally my new best friend, Mystery Kaytee!" boasts Morgan.

I should be satisfied by imagining the injured look on Ella's face when she sees this video, but I'm not.

And yet I keep watching.

And watching.

And watching.

I've already watched this video twenty-six times.

With every repeat viewing, I'm more and more disgusted by the sound of Kaytee's words coming out of the girlbeast's mouth. How could she write and deliver The Letter and a few hours later make a video with my biggest enemy? Doesn't this prove what I feared all along? That MorganElla is a better match for Kiera Tessa Ray than I am? As I start the video for a twenty-seventh time, I realize something far more nightmarish.

Kiera Tessa Ray is a bigger threat to me than MorganElla ever was.

FURIOUS

I'M ON WATCH FROM MY BEDROOM WINDOW WHEN A SHINY BMW pulls up Kaytee's driveway. Morgan blows kisses out the window. Kaytee doesn't blow kisses back and just kind of wiggles fingers at her. I wait until the car is safely down the street to make my approach. Kaytee already has a hand on the front doorknob when I reach the porch.

"Hey!"

Kaytee's face lights up, too relieved to notice how furious I am.

"Sophie!"

I'm pulled into a hug so fast, I don't even have the chance to stop it. I'm struggling to get a breath, like there's an elephant tap-dancing across my chest.

"Why don't you save it for your new bestie?"

"What are you talking about?"

"Morgan! I saw the video!"

"You saw it? I'm so glad you saw it! You were supposed to see it!"

Kaytee wants me to be jealous! I knew it!

"Congratulations, Mystery Kaytee, on To Do–ing without me," I say sarcastically. "You and Morgan deserve each other."

"Stop saying that," Kaytee says. "She is not my new bestie . . ."

I mimic Morgan, "You are totally my new best friend, Mystery Kaytee!"

Kaytee snorts.

"She was just saying that to impress Alex," Kaytee says dismissively. "She thinks they're destined to be together. She's just being nice to me to get to him."

"I don't care why she said it!" I say. "You shouldn't have made the video in the first place!"

"The song," Kaytee says. "Did you pay attention to the song? I wanted you to hear the song . . ."

"I don't care about the stupid song!" I snap. "I care about you bee-eff-effing with my enemy!"

The elephant has asked a fatter pachyderm friend to join in. I sag to the top step and hang my head between my knees. Being furious is exhausting.

"Did you tell Morgan?" I croak.

Kaytee is genuinely shocked by the question.

"No! Of course not!"

"Why did you tell me?"

I focus on Kaytee's pedicure. Painted left to right: red, orange, yellow, green, blue, indigo, violet. The light purple pinkie toe polish is chipped, but otherwise the rainbow is perfect.

"I told you because . . ."

"Because you had to? I was asking too many questions about your past, right? And you know how much I love research. You were afraid I'd sleuth the truth."

"I told you because I trusted you," Kaytee says. "And you promised you wouldn't tell anyone else, remember?"

"I remember," I say. "But do you remember promising that you'd never choose Morgan over me?"

Kaytee's mouth opens, but right now it's my time to talk.

"Morgan will not tolerate someone coming for her top spot. You think she'll just let your past go quietly?" I don't wait for her to answer. "I'm Ickface because I close my eyes when I sing. And Harumi and Sophie are forever known as Chewy and Lickity Lick. Believe me, she'll come up with a new nickname for you that's way harsher than Mystery Kaytee. How does *Killer* Kaytee sound?"

"No one died! She didn't even need a Band-Aid!"

"Morgan is ruthless. She's never stopped by a little thing like the truth," I say. "You should know that better than anyone."

Kaytee's face crumples like a lunch bag tossed into the trash.

"No one will believe you," Kaytee says finally.

"What?"

"If you tell, no one will believe you," Kaytee says. "You lied to me about Morgan, Ella, and Maddy. Why wouldn't you lie to them about me?"

It takes longer than it should for me to realize what's being said here.

"That's right, Sophie. *You're* the one who lied, trying to make me think you were in with the hottest squad at your school. Did you really think I'd never find out the truth? You were obviously trying hard to impress me with your popular friends. And I guess I felt sorry for you, Sophie. So I was willing to let it go."

Let it go . . .

Let it go . . .

Let it go . . .

"Are you even listening to me?" she asks.

Kaytee's face is redder than the deepest sunburn, or an hour-long upside-down handstand.

"Everyone will think *you're* the Ickface rando weirdo spreading rumors about the cool new girl because *you're* jealous. The school is legally obligated to protect my privacy. As a minor, everything is off the record. So *you're* the one who will come off looking like the freak, not me."

Kaytee isn't saying this in a vindictive way. It's not a threat. It's a *warning*. And it would be a valid one too, if not for one detail.

"Are you forgetting about your letter?" I ask. "With your very detailed Life Events Timeline?"

Kaytee's mouth hangs open.

"You wouldn't . . ."

She never thought I was capable of such heinous disloyalty. And until this moment, neither did I. I guess Kaytee isn't the only one who has learned a thing or two about power and popularity by watching from a distance.

"Morgan is determined to hold her spot as the most popular

girl in seventh grade. She'd do anything to eliminate you as a possible threat to her social status. I think she would be very interested in your secret, just to use it against you."

"But you don't even *like* Morgan," Kaytee reminds me. "Why would you choose her over me?"

Before I came over here, I was asking the same question about Kaytee.

I can only answer for myself.

Maybe Morgan will be so grateful to know the truth about Kaytee that she'll include me in her next video. Maybe so grateful she'll make Morgan & Ella & Sophie a new singing trio. Or maybe even so grateful she'll swap me in for Ella altogether! And Ella can *really* know what it's like to be cast aside—just like she rejected me. Let Ella experience the daily nightmare in the Hallway of Doom while I take over the protected spot right by Morgan's side. In Morgan's shadow, of course, but safe.

For the first time in my life, I have the kind of power that actually matters in middle school. I can be the girl who makes the Uncool House cool.

"I'll choose Morgan over you," I answer, "just because I can."

Can I?

Can I choose Morgan over Kaytee?

The moment is anything but triumphant. I've made the mistake of catching Kaytee's watery eyes. I dart back to my house before my own tears fall.

SELF–SABOTAGING BEHAVIOR

I'M HOPING TONIGHT'S DINNER CONVERSATION WILL FOCUS ON THE pregnant teen or another one of Mom's clients. Instead, she turns her attention to Kaytee and me.

"Did you and Kaytee have a fight?" she asks.

The unopened container of Awkward Conversation Cupcakes sits in plain sight on the counter behind her. My stomach turns. I don't have much of an appetite. I'm just rolling chickpeas around my plate with a triangle of pita bread.

"I don't want to talk about it."

I fold the pita in a smaller triangle.

"It's not healthy to keep it all bottled up inside," Mom says. "Too many clients end up in my office because they suppress their emotions and act out in self-sabotaging behavior . . ."

She's not wrong. Maybe if Kiera Tessa Ray had talked about

being bullied, she wouldn't have made a girl exit out a bathroom window. On the first floor. But still.

"I can't help but notice a pattern here," Mom says. "It seems like you are having difficulty maintaining friendships."

She's right. But that doesn't mean I have to agree with her. I try to fold the pita into an even smaller triangle, but it falls apart in my hands.

"Stop playing with your food and look at your mother when she talks to you," Dad demands.

I push my plate away.

Mom gives him a look like *I'm not done yet.*

He gives her a look like *The floor is yours.*

"Does this have anything to do with your squad?"

"My *what*?"

"Your squad. Did you and Ella and that bad crowd decide she isn't"—she pauses—"*fabooch* enough? Is that the word?"

I don't know what's worse, the false accusation or Mom's cringey mispronunciation of "faboosh." I bury my head in my hands. I breathe in and out and in and out through the darkness of tightly clasped fingers.

"The Rays moved here seeking connection and community," Mom says, her voice rising. "And now poor Kaytee is being rejected by the girl next door."

"Poor Kaytee" made a girl jump out a window! I doubt Mom would have much sympathy if she knew the truth.

Ha. The Fullest Truth.

"Sophie, you should know better than to be manipulated by

the hive mind," Dad says in exasperation. "You're the daughter of a liberal academic and a social worker."

I'm starting to think my parents care less about Kaytee than they do about their own reputations as open-minded freethinkers. Why not just let them read Kaytee's letter so they can find out just how wrong they are about her? Or at least that's how I'm leaning until they reveal just how much *wronger* they are about their own daughter when they start talking about me like I'm not even there.

Dad says, "I don't know how Sophie became so *judgmental*..."

What?

Mom says, "That's *not* how we've raised her..."

WHAT?

I'm overcome with a furious energy. None of us are expecting what happens next. Least of all me. I leap out of my chair and before I know it, I'm squaring off with my parents.

Shouting!

"That's! Exactly!"

Shouting!

"How! You!"

SHOUTING!

"RAISED! ME!"

I'm shouting louder than any shout ever shouted out of me. I take advantage of the astonished silence and keep on shouting.

"You judge people all the time!" I point a finger at Dad. "You judged the Rays because their house is bigger than ours!" I turn on Mom. "And you taught me it's okay to lie as long as there's no harm done! Well, guess what! Kaytee and I aren't speaking because

I lied to her and she lied to me and harm is done. HARM! IS! DONE!"

I've never raised my voice like this before. At my parents. Or anyone. And . . .

It feels better than real pepperoni pizza tastes!

Such outbursts are not acceptable in our household. But why not? Before they lecture me, I turn their wisdom back on them.

"Words matter, right? And I'm choosing my words *very* carefully right now, Dad," I say. "Because isn't it true, Mom, that too many clients end up in your office because they suppress their emotions and act out in self-sabotaging ways?"

I can't predict my parents' reactions, but it definitely isn't this: Dad cracks a wry smile. And then, shockingly, Mom does too.

They make eye contact, shake their heads at each other, then start to laugh. And the next thing I know, I'm laughing with them, and we're all laughing together, like we've come to some sort of understanding, though mine is an uneasy laughter because I'm not quite sure what it is.

"She's not wrong," says Dad to Mom.

"She's not," says Mom to Dad.

"I'm not?" I say to them both.

"No," says Mom.

"But you're still grounded for speaking to us that way," says Dad.

RAIN, RAIN, RAIN

I'M NOT ALLOWED TO GO ANYWHERE BESIDES SCHOOL OR DO ANYTHING besides homework until I've written a research report about the importance of critical thinking skills. This isn't much of a grounding because I don't have anywhere to go or anyone to do it with.

I slog to school in waterproof boots, under an umbrella, alone.

Mr. Ray drives Kaytee on his way to work.

I choose stairwell A instead of B, linger at my locker, wash my hands longer than is hygienically necessary in the bathroom. I alter my schedule by just enough to avoid passing Kaytee outside the cafeteria or anywhere else.

If I don't see Kaytee, we won't have to talk.

I'm excellent at not talking.

After a week of not having anything better to do, I decide to check on number 76 for the first time since setting it up. I'm curious to see how much water has collected during this soaking-wet week. The rain barrel was the last To Do I did alone and it's like I need proof that my time, effort, and energy were well spent.

The trash can is right where I left it under the drainpipe in the backyard the day I met Kaytee. Right away I notice a hole at the bottom of the container where the spigot should be. Who knows when the seal came loose and the tap fell off? Any water coming in leaks right back out again. The rain barrel—like the lemon clock, the life raft, and all the To Dos before and after Kaytee—isn't even close to achieving awesomeness.

It's empty.

Just like me.

THE SOLUTION

THE BOOK OF AWESOME FOR AWESOME GIRLS HAS SAT UNTOUCHED on my desk for a week. Seven days is the longest gap I've ever taken between To Dos. It's also the longest silence with Kaytee since she moved here.

I've finished all my homework. I completed my research paper punishment. I'm avoiding my laptop because I know I'll be unable to stop myself from watching MorganKaytee's latest collaboration.

Over

and

over

and

over

again.

I return to *The Book* to kill time. Nothing more. I flip open to a random page, already having decided that whatever task is suggested, I'm committed to To Doing it.

Number 75: "Ask Yourself What You Don't Know and Let Someone Teach You."

Hm. Isn't this . . . kind of vague? And sort of redundant for a book all about learning what you don't know?

By picking up this book, you've already proven to be an intrepid adventurer unafraid to try new things. You've got the grit and determination to get stuff done all on your own. But an effective leader also needs to know when to follow. Put your patience and listening skills to the test by letting someone else share their expertise with you. The less you know about the subject, the better. You're the newbie, not the boss . . .

There's more but I don't need to read on. I wasn't expecting to find a solution to my Kaytee problem. But I think I just did. Right between number 74 ("Plant a Vegetable Garden") and number 76 ("Build a Rain Barrel"). I pride myself on being a quick study. Despite my aptitude for all things academic, there's one area in which I am truly abysmal—way worse than the physical fitness test—no matter how hard I try:

I am terrible about being the right kind of girl.

The kind of girl other girls admire.

The kid of girl other girls envy.

The kind of girl other girls fear.

I'm sick of being laughed at. I am tired of being an easy target. I am done being left behind by best friends when they move on to more popular prospects. I know I have the brainpower *and* willpower to transform myself into the right kind of girl. I just need to learn how. What better time to consult an expert? Okay, so I don't think this is quite what the Awesome Girls Team had in mind with number 75. Any innovator will tell you that inspiration often springs from the most unexpected places.

Fortunately, I just happen to know someone who has demonstrated all the right kind of girl traits—in not one but *two* states. I just need to persuade Kaytee to be my mentor. Knowing what I know, I don't think that will be an issue.

Saturdays are game days for Alex. So I keep watch in front of my window until I see Mr. and Mrs. Ray and Alex drive away. I know they'll be gone for a few hours so it's the perfect opportunity to make my case. Their front door is unlocked—as usual—and I let myself in—as usual. While it's true most kidnappings are committed by someone you know, Kaytee is practically begging to be abducted by a stranger driving a windowless FREE CANDY van. I want to give Kaytee a stern warning, but I remind myself that I've got other business to take care of.

"I've been thinking," I say as I walk into the bedroom.

Kaytee startles, knocking over a bottle of light purple nail polish. If I were Kaytee, I'd get working on that stain right away before it sets into the fibers of the rug.

But I'm not Kaytee.

Kaytee's not even Kaytee.

But I guess Kaytee could make the same accusation against me: *Sophie isn't even Sophie.*

Kaytee ignores the spill. A blob of polish still dangles from the tiny brush.

"I'm sorry too!"

Sorry? Who said anything about being sorry?

"What makes you think I'm here to apologize?"

The purple droplet falls onto the floor. Another stain.

"We both said awful things to each other."

Morgan says awful things all the time. No apologies necessary.

"I'm not here to apologize," I say, holding my ground.

"Then why are you here?"

I can't look Kaytee in the face. My eyes dart back and forth between the two purple splotches on the rug.

"Make them like me."

"What?"

No clarification needed on the unspecified "Who?"

"Make them like me," I repeat.

Kaytee looks flabbergasted, like I must have looked when I learned the secret.

"Morgan never liked me," I say, "and instantly liked you."

"And you think I can make her like you?" Kaytee asks. "Do you know how bonkers that sounds? It's not like I can cast a spell on a voodoo friendship doll made out of leftovers from Kathy's Krafts . . ."

Kaytee's jokes won't work today.

"You are very skilled at being the right kind of girl

264

that other girls like," I say. "I want to be more like that."

"*You* want to be more like *me*?"

And when Kaytee puts it that way, I guess it does sound crazy, considering the circumstances. But . . . yes. Hasn't it always been that way, from the first moment I saw Kaytee hand-walking across the yard? But this is about so much more than popularity. It's about protection. And power. By definition, if I'm part of Morgan's *inner* circle, I can't be in her *outer* circle.

"I just want them to like me as much as they like you," I say. "I want to be in Morgan's squad. You can get me there."

I get a weird feeling like I'm being watched. Judged. The shadow dolphins on the wall know I'll never belong in their clique.

"Why do you think I'm the right person for this?"

"Because you fooled me, you fooled Morgan and Ella, you fooled Mercer and Villa Academy and everyone else since you moved to New Jersey."

"Fooled them how?"

"Into thinking you're so friendly and sweet and not a toxic bully who forced a girl to jump out a window!"

Kaytee's eyes narrow to slits.

"You really don't get it, do you?"

Oh, I get it. I totally get it. What better person to teach me how to be the right kind of girl than someone who fakes it every single day?

"What if I can't make them like you? You'll use my letter against me?"

I purse my lips and shrug like *Maybe I will, maybe I won't.*

Kaytee's warm, welcoming eyes go cold.

"Well, you're one step closer to being like Morgan already," Kaytee says. "You looked just like her when you did that."

I'm simultaneously thrilled and disgusted by this news.

Kaytee rubs a foot across the purple splotches, pushing the color deeper into the fibers. It's easier to focus on the damaged carpet than our damaged friendship.

"Morgan is having a sleepover next weekend," Kaytee says finally. "I'll make sure you're invited."

GOSSIP

KAYTEE AND I AGREE TO WALK TO SCHOOL TOGETHER. LIKE BEST friends do. Both sets of parents are very pleased with this turn of events. Mom and Dad have commended me for my compassion and maturity.

They don't know I said awful things.

They don't know I refuse to apologize.

Kaytee and I are walking in an awkward silence.

"Walkward."

"What?" I ask.

"Awkward walk," Kaytee says. "Walkward."

I want to smile because it's a funny word and also because it's a classic Kaytee mind reading. But I stop myself when I remember the secret arrangement making this so walkward.

We split up as soon as we get to school.

I go upstairs.

Kaytee stays down.

"That shirt really looks cute on you," Kaytee says as we separate. "You shouldn't be so afraid of color."

If I want MorganElla to like me, I have to look more like MorganElla. So at Kaytee's insistence, I've borrowed another shirt. No sequins or toxic embellishments this time, so I hopefully won't go into anaphylaxis. The top is an attention-grabbing pink, bright as a baboon's butt. I don't feel like myself in it, but I guess that's the whole point.

Harumi and Sofie-with-an-F are already waiting at my locker. They've never been so eager to meet up with me before homeroom.

"You're invited to Morgan's sleepover?" asks Harumi.

"How do you know?"

"Everyone knows," says Sofie-with-an-F. "It's on all the socials."

I'm being talked about. This is usually bad. But from the excited expressions on their faces, I'm thinking that this kind of talk is good.

"Morgan posted about me?"

"She posted about her sleepover," Harumi clarifies. "That you're invited to."

The guest list has

0 LOLZ

0 EWWZ

And am I seeing this correctly???

22 GOALZ???

I've never been included in any post that's gotten GOALZ before! That means there are at least twenty-two middle schoolers who wish they were me right now. My plan is already working! I wish I could hug Kaytee for helping me. But then I remember that I'm supposed to be mad.

"No offense," Harumi says, "but why are you invited? You're not even friends with Morgan."

Kaytee's voice in my head rises above all the other brainchatter.

But you don't even like *Morgan. Why would you choose her over me?*

"*Are* you friends with Morgan?" Sofie-with-an-F asks. Her expression is a conflicted mix of wariness and . . . what? Awe?

"Suuuure," I say, unconvincingly enough for Harumi and Sofie-with-an-F to exchange doubtful looks. "I'm best friends with Kaytee," I say with more certainty. "And Kaytee is friends with Morgan."

"And you *were* best friends with Ella before Morgan was best friends with Ella," Sofie-with-an-F adds as if our ex–best friendship works in my favor popularity-wise. Which maybe it does? I don't know how this all works. I could read every book on my mom's shelf and I wouldn't get any closer to understanding adolescent female social dynamics.

I wish Kaytee were here to translate for me.

I wish we could go back to summer when it was just the two of us. No translation necessary.

I wish I wasn't supposed to be mad.

"I was best friends with Morgan before she was best friends with Ella," Harumi points out. "And now . . ."

And now Chewy is in the Uncool House. With us. Where she belongs.

Harumi bites her hair, spits it out.

"Be careful," she says. "Morgan's house has trapdoors, secret passages, and staircases to nowhere. It's like a Dragonologist labyrinth, really easy to get lost . . ."

TUMMYRUMBLE

"Really?"

"No," Harumi says, "not really. But your gullibility worries me."

It worries me too.

WALKWARD

FOUR MORNING WALKS TO SCHOOL WITH KAYTEE.

Walkward. Walkward. Walkward. Walkward.

We don't talk.

Walkward.

Until today.

"You'll have to go to Morgan's by yourself," Kaytee says when we reach the school grounds. "I have a soccer game."

I hadn't even considered that we might go together. But now that we're definitely *not* going together, I can't help but wish we were.

"Wait," I say. "Doesn't that mean Morgan has a game too?"

Kaytee kicks a discarded plastic water bottle across the parking lot.

"She quit."

"Quit?"

"Quit," Kaytee says. "Too much time on the bench, I guess."

This is far less surprising than Morgan joining the team in the first place. Morgan cannot stand being sidelined. Kaytee starts every game, which I'm sure made Morgan's bench-warmer status even harder for her to take.

"So my mom is dropping me off after the game," Kaytee says as we walk up the front steps. "I'll see you there . . ."

And before I even realize what I'm doing, I grab the strap of Kaytee's backpack in a panic.

"So I'll be there all alone? With Morgan and Ella?"

Kaytee stops to look me directly in the face for the first time all week.

"Isn't this what you want, Sophie?"

Eyes, cold. Mouth, tight and unsmiling.

"I . . ." My voice fails me. "I . . ."

I realize the only reason Kaytee is still standing here is because I'm still holding on.

I loosen my grip on the backpack.

I let go.

And Kaytee doesn't hesitate to press forward without me.

JUDGMENT CALL

I ASSUME MOM IS THRILLED WITH MY INVITATION TO MORGAN'S sleepover. I'm finally hanging out with my squad on a Friday night! I'm adjusting just fine to middle school! No social-worky interventions necessary!

As usual, I'm mistaken.

"Hmmm . . ." Mom says. "I don't know, Sophie. Why haven't I met this girl yet? Do I know her family?"

Everyone knows Morgan's family. Both her parents are bigtime attorneys. Morgan's dad is also a congressman. Morgan's mom was president of the Shadybrook Elementary PTO. Morgan's sister is a first-year at Harvard. Morgan is one half of Morgan & Ella, the local singing sensation. Usually I get nauseated just thinking about their partnership. But I'm thinking tonight might be the night when their duo becomes a trio . . . or a whole new duo with *me* as the costar!

"Hmmm . . ." Mom repeats. "I just don't know, Sophie . . ."

Years of working with troubled youth have given my mom a sort of sixth sense for sketchy situations. Well, that and the fact that I called them a "bad crowd."

"Don't you want me to have friends?" I ask. "Don't you want me to be social?"

"I do," Mom says. "But . . ."

"But what?"

But too many clients end up in her office because of poorly chosen peer groups.

"Kaytee will be there," I say.

"Kaytee?" Mom's eyes light up. "Why didn't you say that sooner?"

This seals the deal. My mom wants me to be a supportive friend to Kaytee. And if that means accompanying Kaytee on a sleepover about which Mom has her doubts, that's a judgment call she's willing to make.

She takes off her glasses.

"You know, I hear a lot of sad stories in my office."

I nod.

"There's a lot of suffering in this world. Sometimes I try too hard to protect you from hardship and heartbreak. I don't give you enough freedom to make mistakes."

I nod.

"Your father and I were very unhappy with how you treated Kaytee. But we couldn't force you to change the way you felt. You had to come to it on your own."

She brushes my bangs out of my eyes.

"You've realized how wrong you were to reject Kaytee when she needed you most. And now you're being the true friend Kaytee deserves, not because we told you to but because you know in your heart it's the right thing to do. And that's why I'm proud of you."

Mom pulls me into a hug. And I'm torn between competing urges to squeeze tighter and slip away.

"Thanks, Mom," I say before shaking out of her embrace.

If I hold on for any longer, I'll be tempted to confess all the reasons I don't deserve her praise or pride.

BENEFIT OF THE DOUBT

I'M USING A BUNGEE CORD TO SECURE MY OVERNIGHT BAG INSIDE my bike basket. Dad enters the garage opening a package of batteries.

"It's already getting dark," he says, handing over three AAAs.

He works on replacing the batteries in the taillight while I do the same for the headlight.

"Mom says you're headed to the Constitution Hill neighborhood."

"Uh-huh." I line up the positive and negative terminals, click them into place.

"That's mega-mega-McMansion territory." His tone is even.

Exactly. That's why I'm biking over. My parents cannot see Morgan's house in person. It's four times the size of the Rays' house and would give my dad a quadruple heart attack.

"Who is this girl? How do you know her?"

Dad would immediately recognize Morgan's last name because her father voted in favor of legislation that would spread fracking throughout the state. I'm still not 100 percent sure what fracking is, but I know it's very, very bad for the environment.

"She's friends with Kaytee," I answer. "Kaytee will be there too."

"Oh!" Dad says. "Why didn't you say so?"

I make the mistake of looking directly at the headlight when I turn it on. I'm blinded by the intensity of the strobe.

"You were right about me judging people too quickly," he says. "I'm sorry if my negative comments made it tougher for you to accept Kaytee right away. That's why I'm willing to give this mega-mega-McMansion family the benefit of the doubt."

There's no question where my parents stand on Kaytee and the Ray family. They're all-in on their support. So much so that my dad is setting aside his objections to a family who lives in a neighborhood familiar to him for all the wrong reasons.

My eyes readjust as Dad presses the switch, his face illuminated by the red flash of the taillight.

"You're all ready to go," he says.

Am I?

He places the helmet on my head, then meticulously adjusts the straps under my chin. Not too tight, not too loose. I know most twelve-year-olds would object to such parental behavior, but in the moment I'm grateful for it. I'm like my dad. We're not so good at expressing ourselves. This helmet readjustment is the equivalent to my mom's embrace.

"Thanks, Dad," I say. "For everything."

"Just be safe."

And now, as I pedal away from my parents' protection, part of me wishes Dad and Mom had put up more of a fight.

WHAT I WANTED?

I'M STRUGGLING TO MAKE MY WAY UP THE TWISTY GRAVEL DRIVEWAY
leading to Morgan's gargantuan colonial.

I'm nervous.

For as walkward as it's been between me and Kaytee lately, I
wish we could have arrived together. I can't navigate this overnight
without her help. All my instincts are telling me to GO HOME.
But I know this is my only shot at showing Morgan that I can be
a better on-and-off-screen collaborator than Ella. Too bad I can't get
some same-name inspiration from Sophie Germain. But fighting
eighteenth-century French society for the right to study physics,
math, and philosophy isn't exactly in the same category of bravery
as accepting a pity invitation to a seventh grade sleepover.

I'm sweating like crazy in the hoodie Kaytee bought me for my
birthday. Is the massive front porch lantern throwing off that
much heat? Is this a new stress symptom to add to the rest?

TUMMYRUMBLE
HEARTPANG
BRAINCHATTER
SWEATSTANK

The double doors swing open before I muster the courage to ring the bell.

"Are you just going to stand here all night?" Morgan asks as a greeting.

It's not like I've had a real conversation with Morgan since she invited me. She made it clear she was doing this just as a favor to Kaytee. Ella is just going along with it because that's what she does.

"Hey, Soph," she says. "Saw you on the security cam."

Is Ella still afraid of the dark?

Will I still protect her if she is?

"Hey," I reply.

Am I capable of saying anything else all night?

"Come in," Ella says, even though it's Morgan's house.

It's easy to imagine what Dad would say if he ever set foot inside. *This front entry is bigger than my first New York City apartment!* Some homeowners take this as a compliment. It never is. Morgan walks us past a kitchen large enough for Morgan & Ella to rehearse for their international stadium tour. Morgan sends a text. A second later, she gets a response.

"Okay, I just told Izzy not to bother us because we're filming," Morgan says. "Maybe this time she won't ruin our best take by offering us *snacks*."

I think Izzy is Morgan's nanny. There's no sign of her parents. I'm totally disoriented. Maybe Harumi wasn't kidding about the trapdoors and secret passageways and stairs leading to nowhere. We pass through what I think is a second living room—or maybe it's the family room? Media room? Great room?—there's a lot of rooms to keep track of and they're all full of oversized earth-tone furniture that somehow all looks the same. Whatever room we're in, Morgan hangs a left and starts making her way up a marble staircase to her bedroom on the second floor.

"Kaytee should be here soon, right?" I ask.

"Oh, you don't know?" Morgan asks. "I thought you two were besties."

She pauses just long enough for dramatic purposes before continuing.

"She bailed on us about an hour ago. Said she wasn't feeling well after her game."

"Kaytee's really not coming?"

Oh noooo. This is terrible news. I'm only here because Morgan likes Kaytee more than she hates me. I can't survive this overnight without her assistance—and interference.

"Nope." She turns to Ella. "And *your* bestie is here instead. Funny how that worked out, huh? It's downright *hilarious*."

She says this in the least hilarious way possible.

"What about Maddy?" I ask meekly.

"Dunzo? Don't talk to me about Dunzo."

It doesn't matter why. What's done is dunzo.

"It's just the three of us?" I gulp. "All night?"

"Yeah," Morgan sighs, opening the door to her bedroom. "And *you* are going to make yourself useful."

I turn around, prepared to get out of there without a goodbye when Ella's eyes catch mine. It's a fraction of a second, so brief that I wouldn't have even noticed if it had come from anyone else in the world. But Ella and I have eight years of history. We've communicated wordlessly millions of times, just not recently.

Don't go, Ella's eyes are saying.

Morgan wants to put me to use. And Ella wants me to stay.

Isn't this what I wanted?

Morgan's bedroom is twice as large as Kaytee's, making it four times as large as mine. It's a blinding riot of bling and dedazzle, pinks and purples, predator and prey animal prints. And pillows! So, so, so many pillows! I almost laugh because it's like a parody of Basic Girl 101 bedroom and yet it really is Morgan's bedroom.

Morgan's bedroom also serves as Morgan & Ella headquarters.

I've imagined myself in M&E HQ so many times that it's hard to believe that I'm actually here. MorganElla's videos have improved drastically in quality since their early days, so I'm curious to see what recording equipment and editing software they use. I make the terrible mistake of approaching her computer without permission.

"THAT LAPTOP COSTS MORE THAN YOUR HOUSE!" Morgan screams.

She's exaggerating, but that doesn't make the warning any less effective. I don't touch, say, or do anything unless Morgan tells me to. Fortunately, she's got a lot of instructions.

"Ummm . . . Change the camera angle!"

"Ummm . . . Fix the lighting!"

"Ummm . . . Adjust the mic!"

They're set up in front of the pink backdrop that looks duller in real life than it does on-screen. As we record, I keep hoping they'll make an on-camera acknowledgment of me, Mystery Sophie, the girl behind the camera, lights, and sound. But they don't. Morgan & Ella sing as if I'm not there. They're performing a new Riley Quick song about broken hearts and red lipstick and the chorus is out of tune. The middle part is missing, throwing off the harmony. After the third unsuccessful take, Morgan loses it.

"I'm reapplying my mascara," she says. "And when I get back, you better be ready to sing in tune, *Suckerella*!"

I've never heard Morgan slam Ella with a nasty nickname before. Judging from Ella's wounded expression, it's the first time she's heard it too.

I wait until Morgan has shut the bathroom door before addressing the real problem.

"It's not your fault," I tell Ella.

"I know that!" Ella massages her temples. "The middle harmony is missing!"

Then she looks at me in a way I haven't seen in a very, very long time. Like I'm worthy of her attention.

"Maybe," she says cautiously, "you could fill it in?"

It really would sound so much better if they'd give me a chance to blend in with them. But I do my best to play it cool. I don't want to be a tryhard.

"Maybe," I say just as Morgan returns with tarantula lashes.

"Think you can get it right this time, Suckerella?"

Ella gives me an encouraging nod.

"So, Morgan," I say. "I was thinking . . ."

"If I wanted to know what you were thinking," Morgan snaps, "I'd ask."

I assume that's the end of the conversation. And I'm wrong.

"Well, actually, *we* were thinking," Ella says, stunning me with her use of the inclusive pronoun, "that the harmony would come together if Sophie sang the middle part . . ."

Morgan stops Ella before she gets any further.

"You want to introduce Ickface to Ribot Entertainment? You're kidding me." She shoots a deadly look at me, then back at Ella. "No, you're *killing* me!"

I don't know what's going on with Morgan and Ella, but I don't want to be caught in the middle of it. Without a word, I escape to Morgan's bathroom to get myself together. No surprise that the room's most prominent feature is a floor-to-ceiling three-way mirror like the kind in clothing stores. It's impossible to avoid looking at myself unless I close my eyes.

So I close my eyes.

I have no idea what Morgan was talking about with Ribot Entertainment and I really don't care. She's making it very hard for me to keep in mind that Kaytee is the one I'm supposed to be mad at. Or that Ella is the one I want to get rejected. I might have been seeing things, but I swear she mouthed, *I'm sorry* when Morgan's back was turned. I'm so confused. Is it possible Ella's apology is for real? That we still have a connection? That she still cares? One thing is certain though. I never want to be the "right" kind of girl if it means being like Morgan Middleton.

I flush the toilet even though I didn't use it. I feel guilty about wasting water, but I'm only thinking about self-preservation right now, not saving the planet.

"I feel sick," I say when I return to Morgan's room. "I'm going home."

It's not a lie. I really am nauseated by the fact that I was so desperate to be accepted by someone as awful as she is. As I grab my overnight bag, I catch Morgan muttering something about "loseritis" being "contagious." I assumed she'd be thrilled to have nothing to do with me, so I'm surprised when she follows me out.

"I knew your bestie would ditch us tonight," Morgan says, fluffing her hair. "She always finds the lamest excuses for not sleeping over."

Kaytee's been invited over before? She'd never mentioned that, but I don't know why I should be surprised.

"Ummm . . ." G3 below middle C. "What's the deal with Kaytee anyway?"

Even though it's just the two of us in the hallway, I'm so used to being ignored by Morgan that it takes a moment to realize her question is directed at me.

"What do you mean?"

"She can be weird."

"Weird? Like, how?"

"She never wants to sleep over. And she refuses to share a

dressing room when we go shopping. She never swaps clothes from each other's closets, even if it's just us. Does she have a hideous birthmark or something?"

Aha. Morgan has a hunch Kaytee is hiding something, even if her suspicion is way off in the specifics.

"I mean, she can be *weird*," Morgan says. "Right, Sophie?"

I see what's happening here. Morgan wants me to cosign Kaytee's weirdness. And I could do so much more than that. I could shock her with the bombshell that *no one* at Mercer Middle School could possibly see coming.

"You spent so much time together with your kindergarten arts and crafts," Morgan says. "You've got to know something."

Morgan is digging. She wants information, and for whatever reason—an intuitive power that comes with popularity, maybe, or a tip from the Global Middle School Illuminati—she knows I have it. In just a few seconds, with just a few words, I could upset the whole upper-tier seventh grade social dynamic at Mercer Middle School.

ICKFACE

RANDO

WEIRDO

"Is it a scar?" Morgan presses. "Seriously. What is she hiding?"

I could change everything right here, right now. This is my way in.

I should feel calm.

I should feel powerful.

But I don't.
I don't feel anything close to awesomeness.
I
feel
sick.

AT HOME

I DIDN'T GET MUCH SLEEP. EVEN IN THE SAFETY OF MY OWN BED. I'VE skipped breakfast because I'm still queasy about what happened at Morgan's house last night and what is destined to happen this morning. I'm in The Zone, obsessively refreshing Morgan & Ella's homepage, waiting, just waiting, for their latest collab. Any second now they'll post a new video, a Kaytee K. parody song about a girl puking at a sleepover she should have never been invited to in the first place.

Waiting, waiting, waiting for another dreaded inevitable.

"I'll bust it down if I have to!"

Alex?

"I'll go full Hulk smash . . ."

Alex??

"Come on. Open up, Sophie. I need to talk to you."

ALEX???

I have no idea how long he's been pounding on my bedroom door. I shut the laptop and open the door before he does any unnecessary property damage.

"Your parents let me up," he says. "They asked me to ask you how you're feeling."

He takes a moment to get a good look at his surroundings. And I can't help but think how jealous Morgan would be if she knew Alex was here with me—the loser, the puker, the Ickface rando weirdo from the Uncool House—instead of her.

"This room is like a corny joke," he says. "You know. What's black and white and gray all over?"

I'm in no condition for jokes.

"Why are you here?"

"Because those other girls are the worst," Alex replies. "And you aren't."

"How do you know I'm not the worst?"

I'd like to know the answer. After all, I've been reliably the worst lately.

"You left that annoying girl's sleepover."

"You mean Morgan?"

"*Whatever* her name is," he says. "You're here. And they're there."

The way he spits "whatever" makes it clear that they will never be Morlex, Xangan, or Morder. Morgan and Alex will never be shipped in any form.

"I knew it earlier though," he says. "When you passed the dolphin test."

"The *what?*"

"I gave Kaytee the idea to test your trustworthiness. Like, she showed you the dolphins and how much they meant to her. If you used it against her, she'd know you weren't someone she should confide in."

"Oh," I say.

"You passed," he says. "Those other girls failed. To her face, she was their new best friend. But behind her back, they called her Free Willy on Fotobomb."

"*Free Willy* was about a whale," I say. "That doesn't even make sense."

"I know, right? How dumb can you be?" Alex shook his head in disgust. "It mostly came from that 'whatever' girl, but the other two went along with it, which is almost as bad."

I knew it. I just knew it. At least Morgan is predictable. That's why I'm so certain she'll be grateful if I just give her The Letter. It could be the only way to redeem myself after what happened at her house. Kaytee has every reason to hate me, so why shouldn't I deliver it? And it seems like Morgan is on the verge of figuring out Kaytee's secret anyway. Won't it be so much safer to be on Morgan's good side than bad when she does?

If it's even possible for me to be on Morgan's good side.

If Morgan even *has* a good side.

"You didn't have to lie about being friends with those annoying girls for Kaytee to like you," he says. "She already liked you."

And I liked Kaytee.

"Well, Kaytee doesn't like me much now," I say. "And

I'm not sure I like her either. I don't know the real her."

Alex grabs my desk chair, spins it around, and straddles it. I'm still standing, but he's made himself right at home.

"I know my sister better than anyone," he says.

I still don't know where this is going. But I'm curious enough to sit down on the edge of my bed to listen.

"She's done bad things, but she's not a bad person," he says. "The fun girl who got superexcited about all those To Dos. That's the real Kiera. I mean, *Kaytee*."

I can't believe I'm having a conversation with Alex.

I can't believe I'm having *this* conversation with Alex.

"I blame myself for everything that happened in Virginia," he says.

I am not expecting this at all.

"What? Why?"

"She was getting it really bad from those girls for a long time. I should have stopped the bullying before she flipped." Alex slumps, unable to make eye contact. This is tough for him to talk about. "I didn't notice how bad off she was until it was already too late."

He looks up briefly before returning his gaze to the floor.

"That's why I was so harsh to you when we moved here," he explains. "I didn't know if I could trust you right away."

Kaytee had told me about Alex's sweet side, but this is the first time I'm seeing it for myself. It makes me rethink every interaction we'd ever had. Maybe he felt pressured to protect his twin. Maybe Alex didn't have anything against me personally but was afraid we were getting too close too soon. Maybe he'd watched what Kaytee went through with Gracie and Allie and didn't want her to get hurt like that again.

"How can *I* trust someone capable of such cruelty?" I ask.

Alex picks up a ruler on my desk.

"Should *you* be judged for the worst thing you've ever done?"

I open my mouth to protest before quickly snapping my jaw shut. Alex has a point. Would I want to be forever defined as a backstabbing blackmailer and nothing else? And though I should have understood the message sooner, Kaytee's rewritten lyrics are starting to make sense.

Please see me as I really am,
You're not looking hard enough.
I'm a Princess Warrior, that's who I am,
Not made of monster stuff.

Kaytee wanted me to hear the song in her heart.

And I was too jealous to listen.

"I'm not the smartest guy." Alex taps the ruler on his head, then chucks it back onto my desk. "But it looks to me that you and Kaytee aren't talking to each other because you're caught up in dumb girl drama."

The melody comes to me immediately.

I'm too smart
So I don't

Wanna, wanna, wanna
Play my part
In dumb girl
Drama, drama, drama.

"Dumb Girl Drama" is a Riley Quick song rumored to be about her falling-out with Kaytee K.

"I hadn't thought about it that way, but I guess we *are* caught up in dumb girl drama," I admit. "And Kaytee and I are not dumb girls."

"I'm not saying *you*'re dumb," Alex says, getting up from the chair, "just the drama."

That's a small but significant distinction. I appreciate him for making it.

Alex knocks his shoulder into mine. He's smiling and I am too. After all this time, I'm finally considered worthy of his sister's friendship.

But I need to prove it to myself.

And, most important of all, to Kaytee.

As Alex walks out, I make a note to tell him everything I know about Riley Quick's beach house the next time I see him. As a fan, I think he'd like to know.

INSPIRATION

I READ THE LETTER

over

and

over

again.

Of all the lines in The Letter, this is the one I keep returning to for inspiration:

I was thrilled to have a fresh start, to be the kinder version of myself I used to be.

Consider everything Kaytee needs to accept to be friends with me. Doesn't Kaytee deserve the same fair treatment? Especially after all my lies?

I'm bad at easy conversations. Is there anything useful in *The Book of Awesome for Awesome Girls* that I can apply to this situation? Number whatever: How to Survive an Impossible

Conversation. I flip through the pages, but I can't stay focused on the practical skills I've supposedly developed from To Do–ing. All I can see are Kaytee's hot pink happy-faced signatures on every page, each one representing countless minutes, hours, afternoons spent together.

Maybe one day I'll drive my car over a nail and be grateful that I know what to do with the spare.

Maybe one day I'll surprise Señora Mar-TEEN by saying thank you in Bengali. (Dhan'yabāda.)

Maybe one day I'll crash on a deserted island and not waste any time worrying about how I'll sail back home again.

The Book of Awesome for Awesome Girls gave me the courage to get to know the New Girl next door. Number 26: "Research Your Zodiac Sign." I was eager to write off astrology as junk science, but did the stars know that morning was the turning point for my project? Did the planets predict the moment my friendship with Kaytee became way more important than any To Do?

Without her, the tasks were meaningless.

With her, they, well, maybe meant too much.

I credit the Awesome Girls Team for getting me out of my comfort zone. But it's Kaytee who taught me the hardest lessons about being my best—and worst—self. Now *that* would be a book worth reading and rereading . . .

My chest is pounding, but it's not heartpang.

My belly is fluttering, but it's not tummyrumble.

My mind is racing, but it's not brainchatter.

It's inspiration! I know exactly what I need To Do!

BETTER GIRL

I SPENT ALL DAY AND MOST OF THE NIGHT WORKING.

"I'm going to see Kaytee," I announce at breakfast to make it real.

"You sure you're feeling up to it?" Mom asks. "How's your stomach?"

"I'm fine," I insist.

Actually, I'm better than fine. Way better. I should be exhausted, but I'm feeling awake and alive and as close to awesome as I can get. My parents must be picking up on this positive energy because they're smiling at me with approval. I smile back at them so they can feel good about themselves. But honestly, my decision has nothing to do with them. It's all about me and Kaytee.

I decide that I will walk next door and just be normal. Or as normal as I'm capable of being even under the best circumstances and these are definitely not the best circumstances.

Kaytee is soaring on the trampoline the Rays bought for the twins' birthday. The safety net enclosure is sagging in places. It wasn't installed properly and I'm worried about what might happen if she takes a tumble. Trampoline accidents account for one million trips to the emergency room annually. I never bounced on it because I was too scared. But not Kaytee. She rockets into the sky with her eyes closed.

I don't want Kaytee to get hurt. On the trampoline or anywhere else.

"Hey!"

She crash-lands right on her face.

"Ohnononono!" I cry. "Are you okay?"

I want her to be okay.

She sticks out her tongue. Twitches her nose. Wiggles her eyebrows.

"I'm tougher than I look."

There is too much to say.

I climb through the improperly installed protective netting and sit across from Kaytee, knees to knees. We're well into fall, but it feels like summer in my soul. I practically hear crickets chirping, cicadas clicking, mosquitoes buzzing all around us as I work up the courage to speak.

"I'm so sorry," I begin.

I hold up my hand to silence her like *Let me get through this.*

"I shouldn't have lied to you about all my popular friends," I say. "But from the moment we met, it was obvious you were so much cooler than me. I was afraid you'd think I was a loser if you knew the truth. My parents were never going to give me a phone! I gave myself the To Dos because I was bored and lonely and had no one to hang out with until you came along!"

"Oh, Soph—"

I'm just getting started.

"I'm sorry for lying, and for so much more," I say. "I shouldn't have threatened to show the letter to Morgan or anyone else. It's just, when I saw that video, I got so jealous. And since I'm *finally* being honest, in some ways, I still am."

"You don't have any reason to be jealous," Kaytee says. "We're in all the same classes and eat lunch together, but that's about it. The more time I spend with her, the plainer it is to see that we're not *really* friends . . ."

"I know that," I say, looking down. "I'm not jealous of your friendship with Morgan. Not anymore anyway." I take a moment to make sure I say what I want to say. "I'm jealous that you're better at all this than I am."

"Better at what?"

Her purple pedicure is so pretty. So perfect. I curl my legs under me and sit on my feet so she can't see my unpolished toes.

"Better at being the right kind of girl," I say.

"What do you mean *better*?"

"You're the right kind of girl that everyone likes! Even the girls at Villa Academy liked you; you just didn't like them back! You can ditch Morgan and you'll find a new table of soccer girls to sit with no problem. I don't have that option! I'm an Ickface rando weirdo!"

"You are not—"

"Yes," I say. "Yes, I am."

And that's when I tell her the story I should have told her long ago:

I tell her how I lost my voice.

I'M POSSIBLE NUMBER 45

KAYTEE STAYS STILL AND QUIET THE WHOLE TIME.

I talk.

She listens.

I talk more.

She listens.

I talk and talk and talk.

I apologize and apologize and apologize for my lies.

She listens.

She listens.

She listens.

And when I'm done, she lets me have it.

"Morgan is *wrong*! Ella is *wrong*! You are not an Ickface rando weirdo! I don't want to hear you say that about yourself ever again!"

She's just getting started.

"Cute clothes, long hair, and makeup don't make me a better

girl," she says. "So what if you're not into fashion, cut your hair short, and don't wear lip gloss? Who cares if you never played with Barbies and can't dance? There are so many ways to be a girl, Sophie. Yours is one. Mine is another."

"And Morgan's is another," I say.

"But you don't really want to be like her, do you?"

"No," I say. "No, I do not."

"And neither do I," she says. "You didn't have to lie. I liked you more before I thought you were friends with Morgan. She's a total Scorpio."

I still don't really believe in astrology, but this is a star sign I can agree with.

"Poisonous," I say.

"Dangerous," she says.

"Venomous," I say.

"Obnoxious," she says.

I'm thinking hard to come up with the nastiest adjective of all. "Veganpizzanous!"

We both laugh hard because it's funny.

We both laugh because it's such a relief to laugh with each other again. I hold out my palm. Kaytee takes it. And with her other hand, she tugs on the pink-on-pink-on-six-different-pinks friendship bracelet I didn't have the heart to take off, even when I was furious.

"So no one else knows?" I ask. "I mean, no one else here?"

"No," she says. "I don't want to focus on my unhappy history, not when I've got my future to figure out. I mean, we're only three months into middle school! We've got so much more to look forward to this year!"

She giggles, flails backward, and kicks her legs in the air.

If she can look forward to the rest of seventh grade as 100 percent Kaytee, why shouldn't I get excited about being 100 percent Sophie?

"You can trust me," I say without hesitation.

I know the real Kaytee, the one who deserves only positive moments on her Life Events Timeline from now on. Even after everything that happened with Bee and Allie and Gracie in Virginia, and here with MorganElla, Kaytee still believes in the power of true friendship. And I do too.

Maybe there's one thing I can do to convince her.

Kaytee gives me a curious look as I clear my throat.

Open my mouth.

Open my mind.

Open my heart.

I sing improvised lyrics stuck inside me too long.

Haters are classic plastic,
Hard and fake fake fake.
Our friendship is fantastic elastic
We can't break break break.

Kaytee doesn't hold back.

Before I even get to the spontaneous chorus, she's already on her feet, giving me a standing ovation for a song called "I'm Possible Number 45."

MOST AWESOME GIRL

AFTER KAYTEE'S APPLAUSE DIES DOWN, I UNZIP MY BACKPACK AND take out a rectangular package.

"I brought a bribe just in case you didn't accept my apology."

My gift is wrapped in two different papers: candy canes on one side and pink frosted cupcakes on the other.

"Is it an early Christmas gift or a late birthday present?"

"Neither," I say as I hand it over. "It's a Please Forgive Me for Being a Bad Friend present."

"My favorite kind!"

She's fighting the urge to tear the paper to shreds because she knows my parents reuse all gift wrap. She slides her finger along the taped seam between the candy canes and the cupcakes. She takes her time. I hope it's worth the wait.

"*The Awesomest Book of Awesome for Awesome Girls.*" Kaytee hugs it to her chest. "Did you make this just for me?"

I did.

First, I researched. I picked up time-saving tricks and tips by watching the most highly viewed bookmaking tutorials on YouTube. I was never tempted to check for the newest video on Morgan & Ella's channel.

Next, I gathered my materials. What I couldn't upcycle from home, I found at Kathy's Krafts. I'd earned so many points with previous purchases that I didn't have to spend a cent of my own money! This gift really is priceless, in both senses of the word.

Finally, I worked.

I folded each piece of paper individually, then stacked them in eight sets of four. I aligned the stacks, measured the holes for the binding, and sewed them all together. I punctured both thumbs with the needle, literally putting blood, sweat, and tears into this gift.

The pages are uneven.

The title label is crooked.

The decorative end papers are warped.

But.

For the book jacket, I cut up the red-and-yellow Eco/Echo shirt I was wearing when Kaytee introduced me to the dolphins on her walls. Inside the front and back covers, I glued an oceanic more-green-than-blue textured paper any dolphin could make her home.

This book is us.

I made it for Kaytee because I wanted to, not because a team of Awesome Girls or MorganElla or a teacher or my parents or anyone else told me to. I'm more proud of this wonky gift than anything else I've ever done.

Its imperfections don't seem to bother Kaytee either. She enthusiastically skims through it.

"It's blank!"

"That's the point," I say. "It's time we came up with our own To Dos."

Number 1: Be a Better Best Friend.

"Yes!" She jumps up and down and I bounce along with her. "I love it! I love it! I love it!"

"And I thought maybe we could invite my friends Harumi and Sofie to contribute."

I haven't been very fair to Harumi and Sofie-with-an-F. I need to be less of a bad friend to them too. I can't blame Kaytee for being skeptical about this idea though. She stops bouncing.

"Are they anything like Morgan and Ella?"

Since the sleepover, part of me thinks Ella will free herself from her beastly other half. Maybe I haven't lost her after all. Or for good. But it's too soon to tell. Ella needs to earn back my trust, like I must regain Kaytee's.

"Oh, no!" I reply with a laugh. "Harumi and Sofie are the anti-MorganElla!"

"Then I'd *love* for them to help us!"

And we both flop backward onto the trampoline in a fit of laughter. She's still giggling when she picks up the book and flips it open to read what I've written on the first page.

Kaytee.
Awesomeness isn't always easy.
Friends forever.
Sophie

Now Kaytee is bawling happy tears like *hahasniffsniffblubberblubber*.

"Ohnooooooo!" I'm in a panic. "Did I do something wrong?"

She wipes her eyes on the cuffs of her hoodie.

"We both did something wrong. And we both made it right. That's what matters."

We're making loud and blubbery sniff-sniff noises, laughing and crying and hugging all at the same time. Kaytee and I are best friends making up after our first fight and it's a life-altering moment of messy happiness.

We're two twelve-year-old awesome girls. Forgiving but not forgetting our pasts. Embracing our fullest truths.

ABOUT THE AUTHOR

Megan McCafferty is the bestselling author of twelve novels for teens and tweens, including the Jessica Darling's It List series. All her work is set in New Jersey, where she lives with her husband, son, and two rescue dogs named Louie and Lana, who are much happier when she's playing with them and not tapping away on her laptop. Like Sophie and Ella, she loves to sing and prefers real life to social media, but you can find her online at meganmccafferty.com and @meganmccafferty on Twitter.

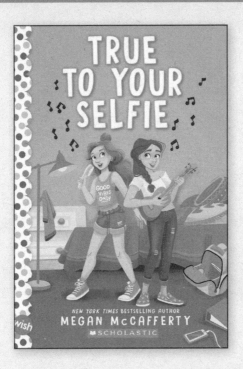